THE IMPERILED PROTECTRESS

Never, Anthea was sure, had a lady ever faced so devilsh a dilemma.

On the one hand, she wanted to save her innocent niece Calandra from a fate worse than death—a proposed monstrous marriage to the thoroughly vile and odious Lord Perry Sterne.

On the other hand, Anthea felt herself yielding to the seductive spell of a gentleman who was as infamous in his own way as Lord Sterne was in his.

What kind of example would she set for Calandra if she violated all her strictures against the evils of such men?

But what kind of regrets would she have if she did not. . . ?

THE WARY SPINSTER

More Regency Romances from SIGNET

THE WARY SPINSTER

by
April Kihlstrom

A SIGNET BOOK
NEW AMERICAN LIBRARY
TIMES MIRROR

NAL BOOKS ARE AVAILABLE AT QUANTITY DISCOUNTS WHEN
USED TO PROMOTE PRODUCTS OR SERVICES. FOR INFORMATION
PLEASE WRITE TO PREMIUM MARKETING DIVISION, THE NEW
AMERICAN LIBRARY, INC., 1633 BROADWAY, NEW YORK, NEW YORK 10019.

SIGNET TRADEMARK REG. U.S. PAT. OFF. AND FOREIGN COUNTRIES
REGISTERED TRADEMARK—MARCA REGISTRADA
HECHO EN CHICAGO, U.S.A.

SIGNET, SIGNET CLASSICS, MENTOR, PLUME, MERIDIAN AND
NAL BOOKS are published by The New American Library, Inc.,
1633 Broadway, New York, New York 10019

First Printing, August, 1983

1 2 3 4 5 6 7 8 9

PRINTED IN THE UNITED STATES OF AMERICA

1

The Viscount Giles Radbourne drove into the courtyard of the Fox and Hounds without any real expectation of success. Mrs. Margaret Taggert had indeed promised to meet him there, but experience with that lady told him that she was as likely as not to have found some reason not to appear. At five-and-thirty, the viscount was philosophical about such matters. It would give him the excuse he was beginning to look for to end this absurd affair. Maggie Taggert was attractive, attentive, shrewd, and ultimately boring. She was also, Radbourne thought wryly, an expert at promising favours she might or might not bestow. It was the general opinion of the *ton* that she hoped by such tactics to lure some gentleman into marriage. Well, Radbourne thought, he wished her luck, but that gentleman would not be him! Maggie was all very well for a pleasant dalliance, but *not* for marriage.

His thoughts thus occupied, the viscount brought his curricle to a halt and looked about

him. The moon was full and by its light Radbourne saw a tall red-haired lady standing with
her back to him and talking earnestly to the
ostler. So, Maggie had come after all—his lordship would have recognised that hair anywhere!
With a grin and a finger to his lips, Radbourne
tossed the reins to his groom and jumped down
from the curricle. Quietly he crossed the short
distance between himself and the pair, and still
the lady did not turn around. Another moment
and Giles was directly behind her. As he slid his
arms around her waist, Radbourne bent down
and kissed the lady's neck. The warm, soft body
in the viscount's arms instantly struggled to
break free. He laughed softly and said in a low
husky voice, "Come, Maggie, don't you know
me? I'm here as I promised! Can you blame me
for being devilish impatient?"

As he spoke, Giles loosened his grip so she
could turn around. The lady did so slowly, her
head held high. Even before he could see her
face, however, the viscount was astounded to
hear her say, "I do not know about impatience,
sir, but I can most assuredly fault you for manners a churl would be ashamed of!"

Confronted by a woman he had never seen
before, the viscount could only think to demand,
"Who the devil are you?"

She met his eyes squarely. "I don't think I
shall tell you," she answered coolly.

A laugh escaped the viscount. "Well, that's
put me in my place, hasn't it?" he said appreciatively. "Tell me, are you always this friendly?"

In spite of herself, the lady's eyes began to
dance, and after a moment she too laughed, and

suddenly Radbourne found himself thinking that he liked this unknown lady very much. So much so that he lifted one of her hands, kissed it, and said, "What I did was quite improper, I know. But it's your own fault, you see, for having such lovely hair and standing here in the moonlight as you were! I mistook you for someone else."

The lady gently withdrew her hand. "Yes, I know. Maggie," the lady said dryly. "Whoever she may be. Don't you think you ought to go inside and look for her?"

The viscount hesitated and the ostler came to his rescue. "Ain't no other ladies, ma'am, at the Fox and 'Ounds with your colour 'air—that I can vouch for!"

Giles gave the unknown lady his most charming smile. "You see? But may I give the same advice to you? It's a chilly night and surely you would be more comfortable inside. May I offer you my arm? I am, by the way, Viscount Giles Radbourne."

He waited hopefully but she merely curtseyed slightly and said, "Thank you, I am going inside, but not because I find the air chilly. No, no, don't trouble yourself to accompany me! I am sure you will wish to wait out here for your, er, Maggie. Particularly as you are so *devilish impatient!*"

And with that, she swept into the inn. Eagerly Radbourne turned to the ostler. "Who is she? Where is she headed?"

"If the lady wanted you to know, she'd of told you, now, wouldn't she?" the fellow answered in sharp reproof. "Now, was you wishing to stable your 'orses 'ere for the night? No better beds you'll find for nigh on twenty miles around."

The viscount stared thoughtfully at the door to the inn. "Oh yes, I shall certainly stay the night," he said. "My groom will help you see to my horses."

Without waiting for a reply, the viscount strode purposefully toward the door of the Fox and Hounds. Before he could reach it, however, a youth emerged from the inn and Radbourne had his second shock. The lad came to an abrupt halt scarcely a yard in front of Radbourne and said, in as stern accents as he was able to manage, "You shall meet me for this!"

It was too much. The viscount began to laugh, first quietly, then helplessly. The boy stared at Radbourne warily, clenching and unclenching his fists. His sense of honour prevented him, however, from taking advantage of the viscount's momentary helplessness. At last Radbourne stopped laughing, wiped his eyes, and addressed the youth. "Forgive me, that was a great deal too bad of me. It's simply that I feel as though I must have walked into bedlam. Will you tell me how it is that I have offended you?"

The young man continued to regard his lordship warily. "I saw you mauling Miss Marwood! You cannot deny it."

Radbourne was amused. "I have no intention of denying anything, my dear young fire-eater. But what concern is that of yours?"

The young man thrust his chin forward. "Miss Marwood is travelling to Bath under my protection and I won't have anyone insulting her!" He hesitated, then said defensively, "You needn't be thinking I'm too young, either, for I've just completed my second year at Oxford!"

"Peace, halfling," the viscount said as he held up a hand. "I had no intention of insulting Miss Marwood, I assure you. It was a case of mistaking her for someone else. Let me also say that I honour you for your, er, earnest defense of Miss Marwood. But forgive me if I ask—doesn't Miss Marwood have any older male relatives to escort her?"

The viscount's charm began to have its inevitable effect on the young man. He was still wary but, on the whole, inclined to accept his lordship's explanation. It was, therefore, rather cheerfully that the lad said, "Oh, I'm not any relation to Miss Marwood. My name is Seabrook. Weylin Seabrook. She's Cal's aunt," he added, as though that explained everything.

"Cal?" Radbourne asked politely.

"She's a girl, but quite a good fellow as far as girls go," Weylin explained offhandedly. "I've known her since I was in short coats. Our families are neighbours, you see. And it's really because of Cal that I'm here. Her father wants to marry her off to Lord Sterne and Miss Marwood said that wouldn't do and she would take Cal to Bath and I said I would go along and, well, here we are!"

Weylin paused to take a breath. Not much of his explanation was intelligible to Radbourne, but he was quick-witted enough to see that the boy might be the means of a closer acquaintance with Miss Marwood and he did indeed wish to know that lady better. The viscount therefore extended a hand to Weylin and said, "No doubt I should explain that *I* am Viscount Giles Radbourne."

Seabrook took the hand, barely aware of what he was doing. "Lord Radbourne?" he repeated. "Aren't you the one who floored Gentleman Jackson, just last year?"

Giles laughed. "It was, I assure you, a lucky punch! I have not dared attempt it since."

"Will . . . will you tell me all about it?" Weylin asked, awestruck.

Nothing could have more heartily bored his lordship. But armed with the knowledge that Seabrook was a member of Miss Marwood's party, Radbourne said amiably, "Certainly, if you will first allow me to arrange for my room and a bottle of brandy to accompany the tale."

Williams, his lordship's groom, was close enough to overhear this exchange. "Milord?" he said hesitantly.

"Yes, Williams?" Radbourne asked with a frown.

"What if . . . that is, should I be keeping a lookout for . . . if Mrs. . . . well what should I *do*?" the groom concluded in a rush.

The viscount considered. A sideways glance at Seabrook showed the lad to be unaware of what the groom was talking about. Hmmmm. Miss Marwood appeared to be a most interesting woman, but she was, at best, an unknown quantity. Maggie Taggert, on the other hand, *if* she appeared, would assuredly provide the viscount with an evening of delicious pleasure. Just recalling the patch of lovely curling red hair between her thighs caused Radbourne to begin to stiffen. "By all means, let me know at once if my, er, friend arrives. I shall be with young Seabrook and you need not hesitate to interrupt us," Giles told his groom. He paused, and there was a distinct twinkle in his eyes as he said softly, "I agree, Williams, that Miss Marwood is intriguing. But even I am not such a miracle worker as to be able to lure a lady into my arms directly the moment I have met her! Particularly when the lady appears to have taken a distinct dislike to me. That will be all, Williams. As for you, my young bantam, I meant no disrespect to Miss Marwood, so you may cease your bristling! I shall not, I assure you, force myself on Miss Marwood again!"

"I . . . I beg pardon," Weylin stammered, "it's only that you've got such a . . . such a reputation and . . . even if you are a viscount I . . . I couldn't let anyone give Miss Marwood a . . . a slip on the shoulder! But . . . but of course if you assure me you won't, I . . . I must believe you."

Radbourne laughed without rancour. "In short, you don't, and are as determined as ever to guard Miss Marwood from me. Well, you may console yourself, lad, with the knowledge that so long as I am deep in conversation with you, I cannot be laying siege to Miss Marwood's honour! Now, then, would you like to hear about Gentleman Jackson or not?"

"Above all things!" Weylin exclaimed.

"Good," Radbourne said with a curt nod. "Then let us go in search of that brandy."

As he watched the pair enter the Fox and Hounds, Williams shook his head. Aye, his lordship had a way about him, and no mistaking that! There wasn't man nor woman nor beast his lordship couldn't charm if he set himself to the task. Right proud of that, his lordship was.

Ah, well, one of these days his lordship would meet someone who could charm *him*, and then there'd be the devil to pay, right enough! Since her ladyship's death, the viscount had often said that no woman would ever put him to bridle again, but Williams wasn't so sure. Wasn't so sure, neither, that it wouldn't be a good thing if some lady did! His lordship was a good master, right enough, and uncommonly concerned to see to the needs of his people. Nor wasn't a better man with his hands, whether it be pistols, horses, or women. But all too often of late, Williams had seen the black mood come upon his lordship, and they'd suddenly go off on a journey somewhere. Usually to nowhere and back again, to London. Thank God his lordship wasn't one to turn to Blue Ruin, or some such, instead! Such men were like as not to beat their servants in such moods. Not his lordship, though. Still, Williams worried. A blasted shame it would be if that red-haired harlot had stood up his lordship again. It would be none too soon for Williams when his lordship gave this one her leave!

Shaking his head again, Williams turned to go back to the stable. There, at least, he was assured of a comforting taste of the home-brewed and the company of men like himself once the horses were settled in their stalls.

2

Maggie Taggert tooled her high-perch phaeton at reckless speed into the courtyard of the Fox and Hounds. Giles must, she thought with satisfaction, have been furious that she had not appeared the night before! All to the good, since so long as he was kept off balance in such ways, his lordship was not likely to feel bored. And Maggie was no fool. She was well aware that her predecessors had invariably been discarded because his lordship grew easily bored. He would tolerate many things, but that was not one of them.

As Mrs. Taggert tossed the reins to her groom, a smile played about her lips. Giles was in for a delightful surprise! Briskly she entered the Fox and Hounds, an astonishing sight with her rich red curls framing her face under a green poke bonnet that matched her green pelisse, all of which matched sparkling green eyes. One sight of her instantly set the innkeeper to bowing and scraping. It was *not* her first visit to the place

and he knew from past experience that the lady
was *very* generous in rewarding discretion. Maggie
smiled again, pleased with her power over even
this unimportant fellow. "A tall gentleman," she
said quietly. "He would have arrived last night.
Alone."

A few more words and Maggie had managed
to convey, without name, a description of Giles.
Equally discreet, the innkeeper managed to convey precise directions to his lordship's chamber,
as well as a spare key, without stating aloud
that he expected her to share it. Indeed, he made
a great show of deciding on the proper room for
her. Another smile bestowed on the fellow, and
Maggie strolled up the stairs, not in the least
embarrassed or hasty.

Upstairs, Maggie Taggert easily found the
viscount's chamber and let herself in without a
sound. As she had known he would be, Giles
was sound asleep and looking curiously vulnerable as he lay with his head on a pillow. Quietly
Mrs. Taggert, known to the male half of London
as the Enchantress, began to undo the buttons
of her pelisse. A few minutes later and she stood
totally unclothed. The viscount stirred, and
Maggie slid under the covers to lie beside him.
Still restless, Giles turned over in his sleep and
his hand encountered a warm mound of flesh. A
hand began to stroke his manhood, and the viscount came abruptly awake. As he opened his
eyes, Giles found himself staring at Maggie's
laughing face, which was surrounded by clouds
of red hair. "Good morning, my lord," she said
teasingly. "I had not thought to rouse you quite
so quickly!"

Glancing down, Giles gave a shout of laughter and drew Maggie into his arms. "Vixen!" he said as he kissed her.

Sure of themselves, her hands stroked the viscount's back and thighs and buttocks. He, in turn, buried one hand in her glorious hair, and the other hand rediscovered her ample breasts, her warm, smooth belly, and moved finally to that patch between her thighs. As his fingers probed her readiness, Maggie moaned, and in an instant Giles shifted his weight and was on top of her. As his manhood entered Maggie, Giles kneaded her buttocks, controlling his pace to match her own. Wild with need, Maggie clutched at her lover's back, her tongue fiercely demanding his. Suddenly her back arched and Giles felt her come a brief moment before his own explosion.

Giles looked down at Maggie with an affectionate smile. "My dear, you certainly do have a pleasant way of waking a fellow!"

Maggie's long lashes hid the sparkle of triumph in her eyes as she said demurely, "The pleasure was mine, I assure you."

Giles laughed again and slid off Maggie to lie beside her. He propped himself up on one elbow and gently stroked her breast. Maggie lay back and watched him. Suzette had promised her a new lotion, one from the Indies, that was guaranteed to make one's skin seem ten years younger. Not that Maggie considered herself in any way *old*, but she looked to the future and was not willing to risk that the day would come when she could not find a protector. Although if her plans worked out, she would soon be Lady Margaret Radbourne and she need not ever fear such a thing again. Ah, the viscount's breath was coming faster now. With a very precise calculation, Maggie Taggert reached out with a shy gesture to once more stroke Radbourne's manhood. This time she was in no hurry and allowed her hands to wander all over his lordship's lean, muscular body. After a while, Giles drew her close and returned the favour. When she began to moan, Giles pulled his mistress up on top of him so that she straddled his thighs. Slowly, with an impish smile, Maggie guided his manhood inside her. "My favourite mount, my lord," she murmured softly.

As Maggie's hands dug into his shoulders, Giles reached up to grasp her breasts in both his hands. God, but she was beautiful with her head throw back, eyes closed, as she grew more and more abandoned! And then there was no thought but the desire to thrust deep inside her.

Later, as he lay beside her, Giles said, "Thank you, Maggie." And he repeated his earlier thought aloud: "God, but you're a beautiful woman!"

Maggie did not meet his eyes. Instead she traced a pattern on Radbourne's chest with her finger as she said a trifle mournfully, "Am I, my lord?"

The viscount raised his eyebrows. What did the Enchantress want this time? "Do you doubt my word?" he asked politely.

Maggie continued to trace the pattern with her finger. "You ... you spend so little time with me, my lord, that I begin to wonder," she said diffidently.

No longer amused, Radbourne caught her finger with his hand and held it in a harsh grip. "You, my dear, were the one who failed to show at our last appointed rendez-vous!" he reminded her.

This time Maggie did lift her eyes to his. "I was afraid," she said. When Giles snorted, Maggie pulled her hand free and rolled half onto his chest as she said, "It's true! I was afraid of how I felt about you! I was afraid you might send me away. I know a . . . a mistress ought not to speak of what she feels, but I love you!" Maggie paused to determine what effect this speech had had on his lordship. His eyes seemed to darken with some unknown emotion, perhaps anger, and Maggie went on in a subdued, almost humble voice. "You needn't fear, my lord. I intend to enact you no scenes. Nor do I expect of you any response. I do not hold *you* responsible for *my* foolishness!"

Maggie had lowered her lashes and now she held her breath as she waited for Radbourne's reply. It was not long in coming. "How fortunate," Giles said dryly. Then: "Up, girl. All this . . . exercise has given me an appetite."

Stunned, Maggie rolled off his lordship and watched him swing out of bed and onto his feet. Whatever reaction Maggie had expected, it was not this. Radbourne might have gotten angry or he might have responded with loverlike ardour, but it was no part of Maggie's plans to have her words dismissed with total indifference. Her green eyes flashed at Radbourne's back as she said with deceptive calm, "Indeed? And if I say that I am not yet ready to arise, my lord?"

Giles turned to look at Maggie, his head tilted

slightly to one side. "Then stay in bed. *I* am hungry."

Maggie no longer troubled to hide the expression in her eyes. "Vardon would never treat me like this!" she warned him.

Giles bent over and planted both hands on the bed. His face was a scarce few inches from Maggie's as he said bluntly, "Then I suggest you go to him."

Maggie turned her head away and said in a stifled voice, "But I love *you!*"

The viscount's voice was very dry as he said, "Understand me, Maggie. You are a beautiful, desirable woman and fully deserve the title of Enchantress that has been bestowed upon you. I have never had a mistress who delighted me more. But I am not in love with you, nor are you in love with me."

"Liar!" she spat at him.

Radbourne shook his head. "Scarcely that, my dear. Oh, I am quite prepared to believe you enjoy my body as much as I enjoy yours—though sometimes I even wonder about that. And I am equally prepared to believe you covet my rank, wealth, and estates. I am sure it would suit you very well to be Lady Margaret. But you don't love me. Indeed I should be surprised to discover that you are capable of loving anyone other than yourself."

"I might say the same of you, Giles," Maggie answered sweetly.

Radbourne straightened and stood, hands on hips. "I have never troubled to deny it," he said coolly. "But what is that to the purpose?"

Maggie licked her lips as she considered his

lordship's face. Abruptly she made up her mind and said, "This! If we are both incapable of love, then surely we would be well suited as man and wife? You cannot deny that we deal extremely well between the sheets. I should, I promise you, be absolutely faithful. But I am not such a fool as to expect *you* to be. If I cannot hold you with my charms, it would only be reasonable to expect you to seek favours elsewhere. What is there to say against the plan?"

"Everything," he answered succinctly. She drew in her breath in a harsh gasp and Giles chuckled. "Come, my dear! Forget this mad notion of yours. You must know I have not the least desire to be leg-shackled again. Not even with someone as desirable as you."

"What about an heir?" Maggie asked with the air of one presenting a leveller.

Giles looked at the woman on the bed and imagined himself with a son whose mother was Maggie. His voice was harsh as he answered frankly, "If you wish to know the truth, my dear, I don't care about the Radbourne succession. No doubt if I died there would be someone to take the title. My brother, most probably, and *he* has any number of sons to carry on the line! In any event, *I* should not be about to see it. Now, are you coming down to breakfast or not?"

"Not!" Maggie flung at him. In a rage she turned the other way and pulled the covers up about her ears.

With a snort, Radbourne turned his back on the bed and hastily washed, shaved, and dressed. His valet, Foster, would have been appalled at the viscount's appearance as he emerged from his room. Giles was aware of this, but he found he simply couldn't care. The devil take all women anyway, and furthermore, where the devil was the coffeeroom?

It was in this foul mood that the viscount reached the foot of the stairs and encountered another woman with lovely red hair. This one was dressed for travelling. " 'Morning, Miss Marwood," he greeted her curtly.

Thea raised fine gray eyes to his and prepared to give Radbourne a sharp setdown. Something about his appearance, however, made her change her mind. "I do not recall telling you my name," she said, but her voice lacked the cool edge it might have had. Indeed, it invited him to reply.

But whatever it was that had attracted the viscount to the lady the night before was gone in the aftermath of his fight with Mrs. Taggert. As a result, Giles spoke rather absently. "I see you are about to continue your journey to Bath. I shan't keep you."

And that, my girl, should please you! Thea told herself sternly. But in point of fact, it did not and, perversely, she found herself saying, "Wait!" The viscount looked at her, rather astonished, and Thea found that her words tumbled over one another as she said, "I . . . I wish to thank you for being so kind to Weylin. I collect it *was* you?" Giles nodded reluctantly and she went on, "He . . . he told me how patient you were, answering all his questions, when I cannot but think it must have been a dead bore for you."

Before Giles could reply, an indignant voice from the staircase proclaimed, "A dead bore?

No such thing!" Radbourne, however, was still in too foul a mood to care about a young man's sensibilities, and said nothing. After a moment Weylin stammered, "Was I a bore, sir? I didn't mean to be. You should have told me to go away."

To his surprise, Radbourne discovered that he was not impervious to Seabrook's earnest, anxious eyes, and he smiled. "No, halfling, you weren't a bore. How are you this morning?"

Weylin responded with a grin. "Fine, sir! I told you we would be up and about early, if you wanted to see Miss Marwood again. But I expect you forgot," Weylin concluded kindly.

In spite of himself, Radbourne winced. "Yes, I forgot."

Giles turned to see how Miss Marwood had taken this evidence of his presumption, and discovered, to his astonishment, that she looked amused. Indeed, Miss Anthea Marwood seemed hard pressed to prevent herself from laughing. "Just so," she said, meeting Radbourne's eyes with a twinkle in her own. "Weylin warned me, you see. I must say that I was all prepared to give you a crushing setdown. And now you say you forgot! That will teach me to be all puffed up in my own conceit!"

Giles moved forward to take one of Miss Marwood's hands in his. "Ah, but you should be," he told her gallantly.

"Should be what?" a breathless young voice demanded behind him.

Lord Radbourne turned swiftly, only to find himself looking down at a very pretty young lady. No one would have called her a diamond of the first water, but she was certainly lovely enough for Giles to instantly predict she would break several hearts before her first Season was over. "And who may you be?" he asked, admiration patent in his voice.

As the girl dimpled up at him, Miss Marwood's dry voice informed the viscount, "This is my niece, Miss Calandra Marwood. Cal, this is Viscount Radbourne. The gentlemen Wey was telling us about."

Anthea's answer appeared to convey a great deal of information to Calandra, for she looked up at Giles speculatively and said, "Oh. I see. I thought you must be. But Wey didn't tell me you were so old."

"Cal!" Anthea remonstrated.

"*Old?*" Weylin repeated, stunned.

Radbourne laughed. "I know I must seem so to you. Positively ancient, in fact! And you are— let me guess—seventeen?"

Cal shrugged and said a trifle petulantly, "No doubt Wey told you." She paused to eye him speculatively again. Radborne merely waited. "You'd need to be old, wouldn't you, to be interested in Aunt Thea? Not that *she's* old, exactly," Calandra added hastily. "But she has been on the shelf for *years*, and it's no use pretending she hasn't!"

Anthea's eyes met Radbourne's over Calandra's head, and at the same moment they laughed. As Cal looked from one to the other, Weylin growled to her to *stubble it!*

Laughter still in her voice, Anthea said, "Calandra Marwood! You'll make his lordship think I'm positively *stricken* in years!"

"Somehow I doubt that, Miss Marwood," Radborne contradicted her. Quizzingly he added, "Would you care, however, if I did?"

There was a warmth, an understanding in his eyes that suddenly left Anthea feeling breathless. Absurd to be so affected by a stranger, but she was. Instead of answering, Anthea looked at her niece and Weylin and said briskly, "Come, children, we must be going. We don't wish to keep the horses standing."

Amused, Radbourne merely bowed to the small party as they hastily bid him good-bye. At the last moment Calandra looked up at the viscount and said brazenly, "Will you call on us in Bath?"

"I don't know your direction there," he told her.

"Laura Place," she replied. "Will you come?"

"Perhaps" was all the viscount would say.

"I thought, Giles," a warm contralto voice said from the stairs, "we were returning to London today." Satisfied with the confusion she had created, Maggie Taggert descended the last few steps and linked her arm possessively with the viscount's. Only then did she say, "*I* am Margaret Taggert. And you are . . . ?"

"Of no interest to you, Maggie!" his lordship said sharply.

Anthea, who had had no intention of speaking to someone who all too obviously was of questionable rep, found herself saying in a cool, composed voice, "I am Miss Anthea Marwood. My niece, Calandra Marwood. Mr. Weylin Seabrook. And although I deplore his lordship's highhandedness, I suspect he is correct in saying we can be of no interest to you. Or to him. Indeed, I should wager he will not so much as recall our existence forty-eight hours from now."

"You would lose, you know!" Radbourne snapped.

"In that event," Maggie purred, "perhaps I ought to take up Miss Marwood's cause and *make* you forget her, Giles. I wager I could, you know."

"By Jove, I should think you could!" Weylin exclaimed without thinking.

Before Anthea could remonstrate, Cal added judiciously, "Do you, Wey? I shouldn't have said his lordship's understanding was quite *that* poor. What do you think, Aunt Thea?"

"I think you are both outrageous!" Thea retorted roundly. "His lordship's behaviour is none of our affair!"

In the silence that fell, Anthea Marwood demanded of herself just why she should care if the viscount made a fool of himself. Naturally a man of his stamp would not be a monk, and one could very well see why men would find Mrs. Taggert desirable! On your way, my dear, she told herself sternly, before he notices that you are behaving as goosishly as any girl in her first Season!

But his lordship was too busy trying to keep a rein on his temper to notice Miss Marwood's lack of poise. Gently he pried loose Maggie's grip on his arm and left her standing at the foot of the stairs. He strolled coolly up to Anthea, bowed, and once more took possession of her hand. "I shall most certainly call on you in Bath," he said.

"Famous!" Calandra crowed.

"Yes, but . . ." Weylin frowned.

"Come, children," Thea said coldly. "Good day, Lord Radbourne. Mrs. Taggert."

As she shepherded her reluctant charges outside, Miss Marwood seethed with fury. His lordship's promise to call on her was prompted, she had no doubt, by annoyance at his . . . his mistress! Evidently he had no real interest in Anthea herself and would never have promised to come to Bath had he not wished to provoke that . . . that female. Men! Well, Anthea Marwood would scarcely be so goosish as to actually look for him. And if his lordship *did* call on them, he would be lucky to find himself admitted! A few moments later, however, as Weylin handed her into the travelling coach, her anger dissolved as Calandra asked, "You do like Lord Radbourne, don't you, Aunt Thea?"

3

Castor Marwood was in an abominable mood as his travelling coach finally came within sight of the Marwood estate. His wife, Eugenia, was scarcely more amiable. As for their daughter Beatrice, she was positively ill from travelling, which was, no doubt, one of the reasons for her parents' foul mood. "Thank heavens," Eugenia said with a reproachful glance at her daughter, "Lord Sterne was kind enough to offer Oglesby a place in his carriage. It cannot have endeared you to him to discover how troublesome a constitution you possess, Beatrice! Not but what Mr. Oglesby is a gentleman and would scarcely cry off now that the engagement has been announced."

"Yes, well, I only hope we may contrive as well with Lord Sterne and Calandra," Castor Marwood said irritably. He had been gazing out the window, but now he turned to face his wife. "It's your responsibility, my dear, to see to it that Calandra understands her duty! Lord Sterne is prepared to come down very handsomely in the marriage settlements, if he can be brought up to scratch. And *if* our daughter don't take it into her head to whistle him down the wind."

"Why should she?" Eugenia demanded. "The girl's not a total fool."

"No, but you can't deny she's a strange one," Castor said with a shake of his head. "What with saying she ain't sure she *wants* to be leg-shackled, as she puts it. And you can't deny she don't respect my authority. I'll tell you what it is! Takes after my sister, Anthea, that's what's wrong!"

Eugenia favoured her spouse with a thin smile. "I collect that next you will say it was a mistake to ask your sister to take charge of our younger girls while we brought out Amabel and then Beatrice? May I remind you, sir, that that was *your* notion? *I* wanted no part of it."

"Yes, yes, well, you cannot deny," Marwood said, hastily reversing himself, "that we are all far more comfortable this way than if some housekeeper took charge in our absence. You could not like, my dear, to leave the girls with a stranger, I am persuaded, and you are forever telling me we cannot keep decent servants."

Somewhat mollified, Eugenia replied, "True, Mr. Marwood. I cannot recall that we have ever been able to retain a governess above half a year. Such flighty creatures they all are!"

"But, Mama," Beatrice protested timidly, "they might have been more willing to stay if you had allowed them to have a fire in their rooms in winter or . . . or occasionally given them a day off or ... or not always been so eager to find fault with them."

Eugenia fixed her second-eldest daughter with a frigid stare. "Pampering and spoiling servants is one thing I cannot and will not hold with. What a notion! Next you will be telling me I should overlook all their faults! What, pray tell me, is the good of that? One would think they would be grateful for someone to point out how they might better themselves. I never spoke but when I wanted to help them, as I am persuaded they must have known! But what can one expect of the sort of person who is forced to seek a position as governess? In spite of your sister's faults, Marwood, she is, at least, a lady. Though why she will not allow me to find her a husband is beyond my understanding. Why, she pronounced me a meddler when I merely hinted at the notion. Me! Not but what I blame her mother for not making the least push to see Anthea comfortably established before she died as some gentleman's wife. It's my belief your stepmother, Mr. Marwood, selfishly wished to keep Anthea by her side," Eugenia told her husband firmly.

"Yes, but so do you!" Beatrice said indignantly.

"I beg your pardon?" Eugenia asked her daughter icily.

With something of a stammer, Beatrice held firm. "When Mr. Stanwick wanted to court Aunt Thea, you wouldn't let her see him. You said she could do as she wished in Bath, but you wouldn't allow her to cause a scandal here."

"Of course not," Eugenia retorted with satisfaction. "A strange thing it would be if I did."

"But it wasn't like that!" Beatrice protested. "We've known Mr. Stanwick all our lives, and how can you say he would *ever* go beyond the line?"

"Beatrice," Castor Marwood said sharply. "You are not to contradict your mother! She knows, far better than you could, about such things. And if she wishes to protect your Aunt Thea, it is not for you to question her. Do you understand me, Beatrice?"

"Yes, Papa."

"Good. Ah, here we are, at home again, where we may all be one cozy, happy family. Smile, my girl. You don't wish to give Oglesby a distaste of you."

From the foolish smile on Oglesby's face as he offered his arm to Beatrice at the foot of the carriage steps, it was to be inferred that nothing could have given him a distaste for his fiancée. Forty years old, he had never expected to fall in love again, but he had. With this girl just out of the schoolroom. Beatrice Marwood was not a beauty, but then, Mr. Horace Oglesby was beyond the age of being enthralled by dashers. He preferred sensible conversation to the mildest of flirtations, a comfortable household to the pleasures of the Continent, and a docile nature to the tantrums of a beauty. Nor was Beatrice altogether displeased with her parents' choice for her. Mr. Oglesby's income was generous, his breeding most correct, and his nature placid. Cal would no doubt be scornful of the fellow, but Beatrice felt that if must be comforting to know she need never feel . . . afraid of Mr.

Oglesby, the way Mama said many girls were afraid of their husbands. Now, if Mama had wanted her to marry Lord Sterne . . . In spite of herself, Beatrice shivered.

Lord Sterne saw the girl shudder and he wondered, for perhaps the tenth time, what it was that had possessed him to accept Marwood's invitation. He was, it was true, on the lookout for a wife now that his mourning for Pamela was drawing to a close. But if Marwood's third daughter had no more spirit or beauty than the first two, then this would be a wasted trip. On the other hand, Sterne reminded himself bluntly, due to Pamela's suicide there were few parents who would even have considered his suit. Sterne could not afford to ignore the Marwood chit merely because he disliked her parents. Nevertheless, he hoped she had more countenance than her elder sisters! But what was this? The butler looked distinctly distressed. Sterne found his boredom replaced by lively curiosity, and he edged closer.

"Not here?" Eugenia demanded indignantly. "But where in God's name . . . ? I don't believe it! Where is Miss Cox? I wish to speak with her at once."

By this time Lord Sterne was close enough to ask, "Trouble, Mr. Marwood?"

Castor hesitated but a moment. It was awkward, to be sure, that Calandra had chosen this time to disappear, but Marwood was not about to allow an eligible suitor for his daughter to slip through his fingers for a trifling reason like that! "Some misunderstanding, I expect, my lord," Castor replied soothingly. "Come inside. And you,

Beatrice! Don't keep Mr. Oglesby standing there when it looks like it's coming on to rain!"

With a slight bow to his host, Lord Sterne crossed the threshold, and Oglesby and Miss Marwood were not far behind. With a glance, Eugenia signalled to her spouse that he was to see to their guests while she tried to discover Calandra's whereabouts.

The Marwood house was a large and rambling one, with a huge entrance hall. Eugenia waited here, by the door, until her guests and family had disappeared up the stairs. Then she turned to the butler and demanded, "Well, Winthrop? What precisely do you mean when you say that my daughter and sister-in-law are not here? Have they gone out calling? Wasn't my letter received? I gave explicit directions that Anthea was to have Calandra here and ready to be presented to his lordship upon our arrival! But there! My sister-in-law never did have the least sense. I shan't be surprised if they arrive home with Calandra in her shabbiest dress, even though I wrote Anthea that she was to have Miss Bixton make up three new frocks for the girl! Well, Winthrop? Speak up! When do you expect my sister-in-law to return? Not very long, I hope, for she must know, after all this time, that we keep country hours here and supper won't be delayed for her. Well, Winthrop?" Eugenia repeated. "Why don't you answer me? When do you expect my sister-in-law to return?"

"I don't," Winthrop stammered helplessly.

"Winthrop," Eugenia demanded, "have you been drinking again?"

"No, ma'am!" the poor fellow answered indignantly.

"Then you have taken leave of your senses," Eugenia pronounced ruthlessly. "Where is Miss Cox? I shall ask her about the matter, though I don't doubt she has more hair than wit!"

At that moment, the rather timid governess appeared. She was out of breath from having hurried down the two flights of stairs from the schoolroom. "There you are, Miss Cox," Eugenia said imperiously. "Where is Calandra?"

"In ... in Bath," the poor woman replied. "With Miss Anthea."

"Bath? Nonsense!" Eugenia said firmly. "You must have misunderstood. My sister-in-law could not have hoped to go to Bath and back in one day. Besides, she knew we were due here today with Lord Sterne."

"Yes, ma'am," Miss Cox stammered unhappily. "I ... I know. She ... she left a letter for you, Miss Anthea did."

"A letter?" Eugenia was astonished. "Let me see it. Anthea must have contracted an engagement for today before she knew our plans, and felt she could not cry off. Though I scarcely see why it was necessary to take Calandra with her."

Eugenia Marwood's confident smile did not, however, survive past the first few sentences of Thea's letter. Indeed, it seemed to that redoubtable lady that, for the first time in her life, she was in grave danger of fainting. Only the appearance of her husband prevented this occurrence. "Marwood! Read this!" Eugenia pronounced in tragic accents as she held the paper out to him.

He took it with a snort. His self-assurance was also short-lived.

My dear Eugenia and Castor,

You will no doubt be furious, but I am removing your daughter Calandra to Bath with me. The news that you intend Lord Sterne as a suitor for her has quite overcome the child and I find I cannot blame her. What devil prompted you to be such a mutton-head, Castor? You surely cannot believe the match suitable?

You will, I've no doubt, hold me to blame for ruining your plans. But I tell you frankly that if I had not agreed to take Calandra to Bath, she would have run away rather than meet Lord Sterne. (You must have known, had you troubled to consider the matter, that Calandra is the least likely of your daughters to allow herself to be sold to the highest bidder!)

In any event, I mean to keep Calandra by me, here in Bath, for the next few months at the very least. My hope is that a small taste of Bath society will make Calandra impatient for her own Season in London. For I do not mean to keep her close at home, but rather give out that she has come for a visit to acquire a bit of polish before her comeout next spring. I've no more wish than you to see Calandra dwindle into an old maid like myself. (Not that I see the least likelihood of that!)

I shall, of course, stand all the expense myself.

The alternative is to return Calandra home

at once, but I will not do so as long as you persist in this folly of encouraging Lord Sterne to pay his addresses to her. Someone must protect the child from such a creature!

Yours,
Anthea Marwood

Castor Marwood quivered with rage as he handed the note back to his wife. "When did they leave?" he demanded of Miss Cox.

"A . . . a week ago," she answered faintly. "The day after your letter arrived.

"Damnation!" Castor exploded. "What the devil shall we tell Sterne?"

"Nothing," his wife replied firmly. "You must go to Bath and fetch Calandra home. I shall somehow contrive to keep his lordship here until you return."

"Anthea won't let her go," Castor predicted gloomily. "Not if she guesses what we're about. And she will, trust her for that!"

"Your sister has no legal right to keep our child," Eugenia reminded him.

"Tell her that!" Castor retorted. "What am I to do? Drag Calandra back here by force?"

Eugenia sighed with exasperation. "Convince her to return! Coax her, threaten her, buy her a new dress!"

"Why don't you go, then," Castor demanded, "if you're so sure of what to do?"

Eugenia merely smiled at her spouse pityingly. "No doubt I ought to," she said. "But I can't. *Someone* must see to Lord Sterne's comfort and, ten to one, if it was you, you would let something slip about Calandra. So it'll have to be you that goes to Bath, and no more complaints."

"Very well," Castor said with a strong sense of ill-use. "But I make no promises. I tell you bluntly that I won't drag a half-hysterical girl back here by force! If I can't convince her, she stays with Anthea in Bath!"

Castor Marwood turned on his heel and walked away, leaving Eugenia with Miss Cox. That timid lady ventured to suggest, "Perhaps it would be better if you didn't try to marry Miss Calandra to his lordship. That is ... since she seems to have taken him in such dislike."

Eugenia raised her eyebrows. "Fustian! Mere missishness! Next, I suppose, you are going to speak of happiness?" The governess nodded, and Eugenia said, her voice curiously softened, "I *am* considering Calandra's happiness. She is not likely ever to have another suitor so well placed in terms of wealth and title. A woman *must* marry, the alternative is too grim to consider! And I am determined that not only shall all of my daughters marry, they shall marry well. You can have no notion how disagreeable it is, Miss Cox, to be married to a man who commands neither respect nor adequate funds. How mortifying to live in a nipcheese way, with not above a single trip to London a year! As Sterne's wife, Calandra would command not only the necessities of life but also any number of elegant trifles."

Miss Cox fingered the worn fabric of her dress and contrasted her situation with that of Eugenia Marwood. Nevertheless, she plucked up her courage to say, "Yes, but even *I* have heard of

... of Lord Sterne's reputation. They say ... they say he is a *beast* in the bedroom!"

Eugenia looked at Miss Cox. "All men are beasts in the bedroom," she replied.

4

Anthea Marwood should have been content. A gratifying number of invitations had arrived as soon as word of her return to Bath had gotten about. She was, undeniably, one of Bath's most popular residents. Some might consider it eccentric of Thea to choose to live alone, with only an impecunious female relative to lend her countenance, particularly when everyone knew her brother had been so amiable as to invite Miss Marwood to make her home with him. But Anthea's breeding and lineage were impeccable and her nature amiable, if rather lively, and she had the entrée everywhere. Moreover, although Miss Anthea Marwood had thirty full years in her dish, she had never lacked for suitors to dance attendance upon her. Except, of course, during those sad years of her mother's illness, when Anthea was, of necessity, kept close at home to care for her.

And yet Anthea was suddenly conscious of a certain dissatisfaction with her life. She was a

woman of remarkable determination. As a young
lady Thea had, during several London Seasons,
been much sought after. Her suitors had been
among the *ton*'s most eligible bachelors. But
when the moment to choose came, Anthea discovered that she could not. Impossible to imagine spending the rest of her life with any of
them. Or to escape the fear of marriage that
sometimes threatened to overwhelm her. And so
Anthea had, to her father's fury, remained single.
Then he died and Thea and her mother removed
to Bath. Scarcely were they out of mourning for
Mr. Marwood when Anthea's mother had fallen
ill, and her daughter spent the next several years
caring for her. Thea was too honest with herself
not to admit that her mother's death had been a
welcome release. Perhaps it was this sudden
sense of newfound freedom that had given Anthea
the courage to refuse when Castor tried to insist
that it was her duty to come and live on his
estate. But with her mother's death, Anthea had
the financial means to remain independent, and
she did so. Her only concession to Castor's outraged sense of propriety was to bring Agatha
Lawley to live with her. And she took charge of
Castor's household when he and Eugenia went
to London to present first Amabel, then Beatrice.
Which, after all, was not such a hardship, since
Anthea was genuinely fond of her nieces.

No, Anthea did not regret the decisions she
had made, but she was beginning to be aware of
a certain loneliness in her life. Agatha, bustling
about the room straightening pillows, fiddling
with the tea tray, could not truly be said to
provide Anthea with companionship. It was not

merely the difference in their ages—twenty years—but a far greater difference in temperament that precluded Agatha from entering into Thea's sentiments. Agatha had not married either, but she never ceased to regret the circumstances that had left her a spinster. She adored her dear Miss Marwood and yet she could not believe that any estate could be more desirable than that of cherished wife and mother. No topic held more interest for Agatha than that of marriages among the *ton* or the royal family. She had been shocked when Anthea returned home to Bath in company with Miss Calandra, and appalled when she discovered the circumstances. "But, Anthea!" she had protested. "Surely your dear brother must know what is best for his own child? And you cannot wish to see young Calandra remain unwed, as we have done? It would be such a shocking waste!"

And that observation was what had provoked Anthea's present mood. She was fond of all her nieces, but it was to Calandra that Thea felt most drawn. The other girls were amiable enough, but in Calandra Thea recognised a quickness of mind and liveliness of spirit to match her own. Qualities that Castor and his wife neither acknowledged nor admired. Qualities that had not and would not be taken into account when they looked about for a husband for Calandra. And yet, what could Thea offer the child? She might indeed force Castor and Eugenia to allow her to sponsor the girl, but outside of Bath Thea could scarcely claim the same number of friends and acquaintances as her brother and his wife. Vouchers for Almack's? Nothing could be simpler for

Eugenia to procure. But Thea might not even find it possible. Nor was Thea blind to the danger that Cal might decide to follow in her footsteps, and like Agatha, she felt *that* would be a shocking waste.

None of her preoccupation showed, however, as Anthea introduced her niece into Bath society. She was cheerful, amiable, and, it was generally concluded, in the best of spirits. Nor was it entirely a hoax. Anthea did, in fact, enjoy taking Calandra about. It was as they were leaving a milliner's shop in Milsom Street one morning that Calandra suddenly darted away and returned a moment later saying, "Look whom I've just found, Aunt Thea!"

Miss Marwood found herself staring at the tall, dark-haired, smiling gentleman behind Calandra and caught her breath. He was even more handsome than she had remembered. He wore pale pantaloons, a blue coat that seemed moulded to his shoulders, and gleaming Hessian boots. His necktie was elegant in a deceptively simple way, his hair brushed into the fashionable *coup-du-vent* style, and his eyes seemed to smile at her as he said gravely, "Miss Marwood! I am indeed fortunate to have found you again."

His eyes seemed to take in every detail of Anthea's fashionable walking gown and bonnet. Indeed, they paused longest on one unruly curl that had escaped to lie along Miss Marwood's slender neck. As she blushed furiously, Anthea finally managed to find her tongue and tell him tartly, "Indeed? I should have thought you would have no trouble in doing so! The Bath quizzes are not precisely known for their reticence, and I daresay any one of them might have given you our direction. Indeed, I am surprised it has taken you a week to find us, and even that by accident, Lord Radbourne."

The viscount grinned appreciatively at Anthea. "My delightful peagoose," he said affably, "it has *not* taken me a week to find you! I have but just this morning arrived in Bath."

It scarcely seemed possible, but Thea blushed even more. In a constrained voice she answered lightly, "To be sure. I had forgotten. Your plans were to return to London that day, were they not?"

The viscount was not in the least abashed. "I thought you would not have forgotten that," he said cordially. "Indeed, I did ask myself if a week was time enough for you to look on me with more kindness than the last time we met. I wouldn't have dared present myself right away, you see."

He looked so meek as he stood there that Anthea was hard pressed not to laugh. She tilted her head to one side, and there was a distinct twinkle in her eyes as she said, "You find me such a terror, then, my lord? A veritable dragon, perhaps?"

"Just so," he agreed gravely.

Calandra interrupted the pair to ask eagerly, "Will you take tea with us this afternoon, Lord Radbourne?"

"May I?" he asked Thea.

Propriety, Miss Marwood well knew, dictated that she give his lordship a cool refusal and later take Calandra to task for her brassy conduct.

Instead, Miss Anthea Marwood shyly nodded her approval of the invitation. Instantly Calandra clapped her hands. "Famous! Wey will be there as well, and he'll be so pleased to see you again!"

"What? Is that young cub still with you?" Radbourne asked with a laugh.

Anthea repressed her own smile as she replied, "Young Seabrook was moped to death at home and . . . and I believe his father felt Bath would be better than London for Weylin to vent his spirits."

"Safer, you mean!" Radbourne interjected ruthlessly. "Where is he putting up? The White Hart?"

"Of course," Thea agreed.

"And he is *not* dangling after me!" Calandra put in firmly.

"Did I suggest he was?" the viscount asked with raised eyebrows.

"No," Calandra conceded reluctantly. "But that's what Agatha—Miss Lawley—says every-one must believe."

Thea intervened. Soothingly she said to Rad-bourne, "He really isn't here to dangle after Cal, you know. It is simply that they have been used to being on close terms. Much like brother and sister, I should say. And for young Seabrook, even though he has been up at Oxford for two terms, Bath is something of an adventure for him." Thea stopped and laughed at herself. "I begin to think my wits have gone begging, run-ning on like this! And in a public street as well." She paused, and the shyness returned to her voice as she added, "We shall look for you this afternoon, sir."

It was a dismissal, and the viscount took it in good part. He had, after all, made a most promising beginning. As Radbourne strolled back to York House, he discovered himself to be even more attracted to Miss Marwood than before. She had chattered rather more than he had expected, but Giles had not missed the colour in her cheeks every time she looked at him. Nor could he forget her eyes. They were a gray that darkened when she was angry and sparkled whenever she tried to suppress that infectious little laugh of hers! Radbourne had called Anthea Marwood a delightful peagoose, but he neither enjoyed mindless women nor underestimated her intelligence. Indeed, Giles strongly suspected that those lovely curls hid an understanding as superior as his own. And no one would have called the viscount a fool! Finally, with a laugh, Radbourne admitted to himself that Miss Marwood appeared to consider him a frippery fellow and was in no great hurry to further the acquaintance. That she was attracted to him, Radbourne was too experienced not to recognise. But he saw no signs of a female setting her cap for him. Rather, Miss Marwood seemed almost embarrassed by her interest in a fellow she clearly felt to be beneath her touch. In spite of his rank. Radbourne had no doubt that she was, this very moment, taking herself to task for not sending such a reprobate to the rightabout at once!

Nor was Lord Radbourne wrong. After reading Calandra a short but pungent scold on the impropriety of putting herself forward so shamelessly, Anthea had read herself the same scold silently. Whatever would Agatha say at the news that an unknown gentleman was coming to take tea with them? Thea soon found out.

For one reason or another, Anthea had never gotten in the way of entertaining gentlemen for tea or meals since her mother died. And Agatha, who was still attempting to accustom herself to Weylin Seabrook's frequent presence in Laura Place, instantly recognised this Viscount Radbourne as a far greater threat to dear Miss Marwood's peaceful way of life. Not but what she was sure she would be very happy if Miss Anthea could only bring herself to accept one of her more genteel suitors. But not one of those suitors would have dreamed of so intruding into dear Anthea's household as this . . . this stranger was doing!

As patiently as she was able, Thea listened to Agatha's objections. But she was adamant. His lordship *was* coming to tea. "And I really *do* think my credit may survive such wild behaviour," Thea told her companion in exasperation.

Agatha tittered. "My dear Anthea! Such a love of funning you have! Still, I am persuaded your brother—"

But this was too much for Anthea. "It is none of Castor's affair!" she snapped, her eyes glittering dangerously. "And if you are so distressed by my plans, I give you leave to take the afternoon off, Agatha."

But this, in turn, was too much for Agatha. Desert her dear Miss Marwood? She could not and would not do such a thing! The very notion was repugnant to her. After all, she had been hired to lend propriety to dear Anthea's household!

Thus it was that when the viscount arrived,

punctually at quarter to four, he had the doubtful pleasure of finding Miss Agatha Lawley alone
in the drawing room. A few minutes later,
fortunately, Miss Anthea Marwood appeared.
That few minutes, however, was sufficient for
Miss Lawley to subject his lordship to such an
exhaustive query on his antecedents, number of
properties, current social entanglements, and
whatnot that Radbourne was hard put to be
polite. The look he gave Miss Marwood was so
speaking, in fact, that she took pity on him and
sent Agatha out of the room to check on Calandra.
Radbourne's first words to Anthea were, "Good
God! Is that woman always about you? How do
you stand it?"

Anthea laughed but shook her head at him.
"You have no notion, my lord," she told him
sternly, "how much I have to be grateful to
Agatha for!"

"Companionship, no doubt!" Giles said wither-
ingly.

"You must know," Thea said, firmly ignoring
him, "that if I had not found someone like Miss
Lawley, I should have had to live with my
brother, Castor. And that, I was determined not
to do! As a man, you are allowed to do as you
wish. If you choose to live alone, no one thinks
it odd. But if I did so, any number of people
would cut me directly. I should be thought shockingly fast or hopelessly eccentric. I have no wish
to be known as either. If . . . if I do not find
Agatha's conversation altogether . . . fascinating,
at least she does not dare try to rule my life.
Even a limited independence is better than
none!"

Radbourne had no opportunity to answer. Appalled at the impropriety of dear Miss Marwood receiving a gentleman alone, Agatha had all but dragged Calandra from her room. And, at the same moment, Weylin arrived as well, and the elegantly appointed drawing room seemed suddenly full of people. Seabrook, moreover, scarcely had eyes for anyone other than the viscount. "Sir! You're here! Where are you putting up? How long will you stay? Did you bring your own cattle to Bath? That bang-up set of grays you had at the inn?"

"York House. I don't know how long I shall be staying. And no, I did not bring my grays. I drove my chestnuts instead," Radbourne replied coolly. He paused, then added, "And no, you may not drive them."

Weylin took the setdown in good part and turned, cheerfully enough, to greet Anthea. Miss Lawley startled Radbourne by graciously informing him, "My dearest Papa was used to say that it was the height of folly to entrust young men with teams they cannot possibly handle."

From the expression on Weylin's face, Radbourne inferred that this was not the first time the boy had been privileged to hear one of Miss Lawley's pronouncements. Fortunately, she did not seem to expect a reply. Agatha, in fact, seemed quite content to occupy herself with serving everyone from the tea tray that had now appeared.

As Calandra and Weylin settled themselves on two chairs near the window, Giles observed to Anthea, "She's very pretty. I collect you'll have your hands full so long as you find her in your care!"

As Thea's eyes rested on Calandra, they softened. "She is a pretty child, isn't she?"

"I find it astonishing her father should even think of marrying her to Lord Sterne." At Thea's startled look, Radbourne said apologetically, "I'm sorry. Young Seabrook told me."

"I see." Anthea hesitated. By all the dictates of propriety, she ought not to confide in this man. Her own intelligence, moreover, told her that the viscount's character was not altogether admirable. But when she looked at Radbourne, propriety and cool, rational judgment were forgotten in the certain knowledge that in this, at least, she could trust him. "No doubt you are wondering about my part in this," Anthea said, meeting his eyes, "but when I learned my brother's plans, I felt I could not allow such a thing! And I could think of nothing for it but to bring Cal here. At the very least, I hope it will give my brother pause." She looked up at the viscount. "Is my dislike of Lord Sterne mere prejudice? Or am I right to think him not . . . not the thing for Calandra? You must know his lordship, certainly better than I do."

Radbourne's tone was grim as he answered. "I do know him and can tell you frankly that I would never allow him near a niece of mine. But how do you come to know him at all? Or is it merely his reputation that made you act as you did?"

Anthea shook her head, her colour rising. "In . . . in my first Season I . . . I met his lordship once at a Ball. He . . . he managed to . . . to trap

me in a corner and . . . and force a . . . kiss. My
father told me I . . . I refined too much upon the
matter." Anthea paused to draw a deep breath,
then added defiantly, "No doubt you are thinking me unbearably missish to be overset by a
mere kiss. But it wasn't the kiss. It was the
certainty I felt that Lord Sterne had . . . had
done so only to frighten me; that he took great
pleasure in my fear! And I will not have him
frightening Calandra."

Giles looked at Thea with a small smile. "I do
not think you missish," he said. "I think you
delightful instead!"

Thea set down her teacup with a sharp breath.
There was more than a hint of impatience in her
voice as she said, "Lord Radbourne, ever since
we met, you have been paying me absurd compliments! Why? What possible interest can I hold
for you, save that I faintly resemble your current mistress? I am a stranger to you and I have
neither fortune, nor youth, nor beauty to recom-
mend me to you."

"A veritable antidote?" Radbourne suggested
dryly.

"No, of course not!" Anthea retorted. She
looked down at her hands and spoke with a
frown. "But I will not be other than honest with
myself. I have never lacked for suitors, but . . ."

"But still you don't understand me?" Giles
asked gently. Anthea nodded, and he shrugged
his broad shoulders. "No more do I understand
myself. You do not *seem* a stranger to me, and
unaccountably I feel I might tell you anything,
Miss Marwood, and you would understand. Does
that seem an absurd fancy to you?"

Anthea shook her head. "No, for I've felt that too," she said quietly.

Radbourne's deep voice compelled Thea to look at him as he said, "I don't offer Spanish coin, you know! Not to you. In a week I may be telling you to go to the devil! But whatever I say, it will be honest."

In spite of herself, Anthea gave a gurgle of laughter. Agatha, her attention attracted, favoured Thea with an indulgent smile and told Lord Radbourne, "My dearest Papa was used to say that a little laughter brightened the gloomiest of houses! Not, of course, that I mean to say *this* house could ever be gloomy, situated as it is to catch the morning sun and favoured by my dear Miss Marwood's presence."

"*Which* Miss Marwood?" Weylin asked with an impish smile.

Hastily Calandra intervened before Agatha could utter a reproof. "Aunt Thea! Wey tells me there are Saxon fortifications nearby. Lansdown, I believe. Could I go with him to see them? I could borrow your mare."

Anthea looked at her niece helplessly. "I wish I could allow it! But to ride such a distance alone, unchaperoned, with Weylin—"

Weylin snorted. "Lord, Miss Marwood, you know I ain't going to go beyond the line with Cal! It would be like kissing my sister!"

"You know very well I didn't mean *that*," Thea told him sternly. "It's the Bath gossips I'm thinking of."

"Well, come along with us," Calandra suggested generously. "We promise not to set too fast a pace for you."

Anthea favoured her niece with a withering smile. Before she could speak, however, Lord Radbourne did, astonishing everyone. "Won't you go along with them?" he asked her coaxingly. "And allow me to join the party? I've never seen the fortifications either, you know."

Thea looked at Radbourne, her lower lip caught between her teeth. "Very well," she said after a moment. "When shall we go?"

"I am not altogether certain my dearest Papa would have approved such an expedition," Agatha observed cautiously. "It might look too particular, you know. He was used to say, however, that the early-morning hours were best for riding."

"Well, we wouldn't wish to altogether contradict Papa," the viscount replied gravely. "We shall most certainly go in the morning. Tomorrow, perhaps?"

Casting a reproachful glance at Calandra, who was giggling, Anthea said, "Very well. Tomorrow morning. Eight o'clock? Unless the children have an objection?"

The children did not, except perhaps to this form of address, and the matter was arranged in a trice. Soon after, Lord Radbourne took his leave and Weylin eagerly accompanied him. It was beyond everything great, he told Calandra, that a top-of-the-trees fellow like his lordship should take an interest in a fellow like himself!

5

To Calandra's relief, the morning was a fair one,
and by the time Weylin and Viscount Radbourne
arrived, she was more than ready. Not only had
Calandra donned her riding habit, she had con-
sumed an ample breakfast and found time to
rearrange her hair three or four times. Anthea
was far less eager. She had, in fact, risen with
the question in her mind of whether or not to
cancel the expedition. Whatever had possessed
her to agree to an outing that must surely encourage his lordship's attentions? It was madness! However *eligible* he might be, Lord Radbourne was, after all, an acknowledged rake.
Anthea knew, from acquaintances with daughters,
that society had long since despaired of seeing
his lordship remarry. Her own instincts, moreover,
informed her that here was a man who had long
since ceased to greatly consider the wishes of
others. But the thing which disturbed Anthea
the most was the absurd warmth she felt each
time her eyes met those of the viscount. One

look at Calandra's face, however, made it clear
to Anthea that cancelling the proposed expedition was out of the question. Anthea consoled
herself with the reminder that she need not see
his lordship after today, unless she chose to do
so.

Had Anthea but known it, Radbourne had much
the same doubts as she did. It was not in his
nature to engage in such pointed pursuit of a
woman except when it was clearly understood,
by both sides, that a brief affair was all that was
intended. What the devil, he asked himself while
shaving, was he doing?

Weylin, like Calandra, was untroubled by such
considerations. He simply was eager to see the
fortifications. Barely had greetings been exchanged in front of Miss Marwood's house, and
leave taken of Miss Lawley, before he was urg-
ing Calandra to mount and demanding of Miss
Marwood precise directions for Lansdown. "But
. . . but I don't know where the ruins are!" Anthea
protested. "I thought *you* did, Weylin."

"How should I?" Seabrook retorted. "I've never
been to Bath before. And you've lived here for
ages. I just assumed you would know. You said
you go out riding often!"

"And I also said I had never visited the ruins!"
Anthea retorted with some asperity.

At this point the viscount intervened. He
cleared his throat loudly and waited for Weylin
and Miss Marwood to give him their attention.
Then he said, "*I* took the liberty of asking for
directions at York House and believe I can undertake to bring us there and back."

Anthea did not trouble to hide her relief. Weylin was even more vocal in his approval. "By Jupiter, I knew you were a Trojan, sir! How far is it? Did they tell you what we might expect to find? Is it a common spot for visitors? I shouldn't like to go there simply to find the place overrun with curiosity-seekers!"

Lord Radbourne was able to reassure Weylin on the salient points, although he confessed that he had not thought to ask for a detailed description of the ruins. "I thought we might prefer to judge them for ourselves," Radbourne explained meekly.

Weylin was quick to assure the viscount that he saw nothing to cavil at in this point of view and called on Miss Marwood to agree. "Don't you think it the greatest good fortune his lordship came along?" Weylin asked her earnestly.

"Why, yes," Anthea said coolly, her eyes on the street ahead. "I certainly see that we should have found ourselves in the briars if he hadn't. I cannot think how it comes about that, in all the years I have lived here, I have never thought to equip myself with a guidebook. Shockingly improvident of me, for something tells me I should have foreseen just such an occasion as this!"

"Frankly, I am happy that you did not, for it makes me indispensable to this expedition," Radbourne replied amiably. Startled, Anthea looked up to discover that his lordship had taken advantage of her preoccupation with the local traffic to draw his horse up next to hers. As she looked at him, Radbourne smiled at Miss Marwood and directed her to look to what she was about.

"You almost ran down that urchin, you know," he told her kindly. Anthea did not trust herself to answer, but looked resolutely away and Radbourne went on, "I wonder who it was that so foolishly declared all redheads to be fiery-tempered? For my part, I seem to be greeted far more often by a cold shoulder than a warm welcome from you. But perhaps it is my fault and if I were only to give you the opportunity, you would surround me with flames of passion?" Radbourne concluded hopefully.

Miss Anthea Marwood turned to Lord Radbourne with the intention of informing him just what she thought of such outrageous nonsense! But she could not. For when her eyes met his, Thea discovered that Giles was looking at her as though he fully expected her to share his amusement at his words. And the worst part of it was, Anthea told herself angrily as she hastily tore away her gaze, she did! Stiffly she said aloud, "I would prefer it, sir, if you did not say such things to me."

"All right," Radbourne said meekly. Anthea shot him a suspicious glance and, too late, realised her mistake as he went on affably, "What *would* you like me to say to you? We've already agreed that Spanish coin won't do. I've always prided myself on my conversation, you see, and now you've put paid to that!" he concluded mournfully.

First Thea's shoulders shook, then a dimple in her cheek quivered, and finally she laughed outright. "You are impossible!" she told the viscount roundly.

"Yes, ma'am," he agreed meekly.

"You don't in the least deceive me," Anthea told him severely. "You are the most . . . most complete hand, as Weylin would say! Which is, I suppose," she said with a sigh, "why I like you so much. And I shouldn't!"

"Why not?" Giles asked her. "Are only sober people respectable?"

Anthea regarded him ruefully. "It sometimes seems that way, doesn't it? I have always had it drummed into me that I ought to be more steady and sober. Castor is forever saying that levity will be the ruination of me."

"For someone who could contemplate the marriage of one of his daughters to Lord Sterne, it is the outside of enough for Marwood to say such a thing to you!" Radbourne answered shortly. Anthea looked at him in surprise and he said, "Forgive me. Perhaps *I* ought not to say such things of your brother. But it does put me in a puzzle how anyone who is so vehement in his claims to be such a high stickler could allow such a match! And futhermore to criticise you!"

"Ah, but you don't understand," Thea told him in tolerable imitation of Eugenia Marwood's manner. "It is one thing for a young girl to very properly obey her parents' wishes in the matter of marriage. If she does so, there can be no question of scandal, whatever the reputation of the groom. But for any female to please herself, on any matter, without regard for the wishes of her family, is behaviour which must outrage every feeling! Such a female has sunk herself beyond reproach and must excite digust in everyone who sees her as the most selfish of creatures."

"Surely she cannot have said that to you," Radbourne protested.

"But I assure you she did," Anthea retorted. "For my own good, of course!"

"I collect," Radbourne said dryly, "that you are *not* the favourite of your family. I wonder they dare place their daughters in your care!"

Thea laughed at him. "Do you? It had me in a puzzle, too, until I realised the truth of the matter. It suits my brother and his wife quite well to have me handy to take charge of their household whenever they choose to flit off to London. Lord Sterne is acceptable for the same reason. Money. My brother and his wife are the greatest nipfarthings imaginable! They are well able to afford a housekeeper but will not. Though to own the truth," she added reflectively, "that isn't the whole of the matter. My sister-in-law, Eugenia, has not the . . . the most conciliating of natures."

Radbourne grinned appreciatively. "And you call *me* outrageous!" he told her with an air of reproach.

Thea looked at him ruefully. "I know, my wretched tongue! But you will not . . . will not regard anything I have said? If you were anyone else I would not have . . . have spoken so freely." Giles was looking at Thea politely, and she added crossly, "And why the devil I *should* find myself so frank with you is beyond me!"

Radbourne only laughed and looked about him, for by this time the party had passed beyond the outskirts of Bath. Weylin and Calandra promptly took this as a signal to draw abreast of their elders. "Which way now, sir?" Weylin asked eagerly.

"This way," Radbourne replied, pointing. He then added, "I hope."

But Weylin would not allow such a cowardly doubt. He was not so foolish as to actually snort his derision, but Lord Radbourne seemed to realise that he had fallen in Weylin's estimation, for he began to discuss the history of the area. Calandra and Thea fell in with one another.

"I like him, don't you?" Calandra asked her aunt.

Rather startled out of her reverie, Thea looked at Cal. "Who?" she asked. "Weylin? Of course I do."

Calandra grinned at her aunt and said sternly, "That is *not* who I mean, and well you know it, my dearest of aunts! I meant Lord Radbourne."

"To be sure," Anthea said dryly. "Your liking for his lordship has been quite evident! Must you be so forward? It really is not the thing, you know. What if he should take offense?"

Calandra hesitated before answering. When she finally did, she spoke with an unaccustomed diffidence. "But I don't think he will, Aunt Thea. I don't know why, but one feels as if he quite understands. Yes, and enters into all of one's sentiments, as well, or at the very least would never roast one for them."

With dismay, Anthea wondered if her niece were in danger of losing her heart to Lord Radbourne. The viscount might well, she knew, seem a romantic figure to an impressionable young girl. So it was with some restraint that

Thea replied, "Why yes, one does feel that. But, Cal, you *do* realise his ... his lordship is not generally accounted to ... to be likely to marry again?"

Calandra distinctly snorted. "Oh, pooh! As though you would care! Or *are* you hanging out for a husband?"

"No, of course not!" Anthea replied. "I ... I am well content with my lot. But I never looked for you to follow in my footsteps."

"Well, but that is my affair, is it not?" Calandra asked reasonably. Suddenly she laughed. "You look so serious, Aunt Thea. Why?"

Miss Marwood abandoned all prudence and spoke frankly. "I am worried that you may be hurt, Cal. Lord Radbourne is an accomplished flirt, far more experienced than you, and—"

Calandra cut short her aunt with another shout of laughter. "Did you think I meant I was after his lordship? How absurd! He's by far too old for me. I only encouraged him to call because he seemed precisely the sort of man who would appeal to you, Aunt Thea. And he does, doesn't he?" she asked anxiously. "I mean, he seems to care no more for convention than you do. Weylin says that Radbourne is everywhere received and generally considered to be good *ton*, so he can't really go about breaking rules all the time. But one has the feeling he chooses to follow convention and could just as easily choose not to. *Do* you know what I mean, Aunt Thea?"

Slowly Miss Marwood nodded. "Yes, I think I do. And I shouldn't say so, but you are quite right that that is part of what appeals to me about him. What has me in a puzzle is why he should bother with me, however!"

Calandra felt this to be an absurd question and favoured her aunt with an affectionate shake of her head. A moment later she said impulsively, "Let's challenge them to a race, shall we?"

As Calandra didn't wait for an answer but immediately urged her horse to a gallop, Anthea had no choice but to follow suit. Unfortunately, the conclusion drawn by Weylin and Radbourne was that the ladies' horses had run away with their riders. So a moment later there were four horses galloping madly across the fields.

Giles urged his bay forward until he drew abreast of Miss Marwood's gray mare. Anxiously he reached out and seized the mare's bridle and forced both horses to slow. When he had brought them to a halt, Giles perceived that Miss Marwood was regarding him with the liveliest astonishment, but Radbourne found he was too angry to consider what that might mean. "Are you all right?" he demanded. "What the devil possessed you to ride a horse you couldn't manage?"

Affronted, Anthea retorted coldly, "I can."

"Of course. You always ride hell-bent-for-leather?" he suggested sarcastically.

"Calandra and I were racing," Anthea retorted, forgetting that it had not been her choice.

"Really?" he asked icily. "And is that the sort of example you choose to set for her? If so, you are even less fitted to care for the child than I thought."

Anthea smiled at him sweetly. "I was not aware that that was in any way your concern," she said. "Moreover, although you might question my judgment in racing Calandra, I cannot see what other possible objection there can be to my taking charge of her."

Once more Radbourne's face was transformed by his smile. "Your youth," he explained succinctly.

Anthea looked at him blankly. "My *youth*? You must have windmills in your head! I *am* above thirty, you know," she said with as much dignity as she could muster.

"What a bouncer!" Radbourne retorted.

In spite of herself, Thea grinned. "Well, I am," she said. "By two months, at any rate. But do be serious! I collect you do object to my taking charge of Cal, and I cannot understand why."

"I meant it when I said my objection was your youth," Radbourne repeated calmly. "You ought to be out dancing yourself instead of chaperoning that child. How you have escaped marriage thus far is beyond me and there is no reason why you should continue to do so! Why aren't you married?" he concluded outrageously.

"You needn't think I didn't take!" Anthea bristled. "I came out the same year as your wife, Clarissa Lambert, and even if you had no eyes for anyone else, there were gentlemen who did. I simply didn't wish to marry any of them."

"And I suppose you then proceeded to bury yourself here in Bath?" he asked indignantly. "What an appalling waste!"

"Actually, I had several Seasons in London," Anthea corrected him gently. "But it's true that I withdrew to Bath afterwards. Probably about the time you came out of mourning for your wife, in fact. I remember that she was very beautiful."

"Very," Radbourne agreed curtly. He smiled at Thea, a trifle wistfully. "Do you imagine I've been wearing the willow for her? I haven't, you know. Clarissa was very beautiful and also very uninterested in me, once we were married. Within a year, from one excuse or another, I found myself banished from the bedroom and her affairs generally. She was very much afraid, you see, of childbirth and losing her figure by breeding. Nothing mattered to her but the admiration of gentlemen, preferably not her husband! Clarissa finally killed herself by riding neck-or-nothing at a fence her horse could not possibly have managed. And why the devil I'm telling *you* all this, I can't imagine!" he concluded roundly. "But that is why you cannot expect me to stand by while you ride madly and risk such a tumble!"

Anthea barely heard his last few words. Her thoughts were, instead, on the proud young man who had been faced with a wife who did not want him. No wonder Lord Radbourne had never remarried! Abruptly Radbourne's rough voice dragged Anthea back to the present. "Will you stop staring at me like that, Miss Marwood?" he asked with some asperity. "Your niece and her friend are waiting for us, and I, for one, do not choose to sit here all day!"

Hastily Anthea recollected herself and managed to answer him calmly enough. "Neither do I, sir. Which way do we go now?"

If there was a certain constraint between the pair, it could not last long in the face of such a perfect day. Which was fortunate, Radbourne told himself later as he watched Miss Marwood tether her horse near the ruins. If ever there was a bubbleheaded way to begin an affair! I am not, he reminded himself grimly, usually so maladroit. No, another inner voice agreed, and neither do you usually encounter women like Miss Marwood.

But there was no time to brood upon the matter. Young Seabrook was determined to engage the viscount in a discussion of military tactics invaders might have used. It was not precisely what his lordship had envisioned when he offered to accompany the expedition, but he nevertheless amiably obliged Weylin.

Anthea and Calandra resolutely declined to traipse all over the ruins, contenting themselves with the easier portions to reach. Eventually the party found itself back in Bath. Upon reaching the house in Laura Place, the gentlemen reluctantly prepared to take their leave of the ladies. Before either Calandra or Thea could dismount, however, the door of Miss Marwood's house was flung open and Castor Marwood clattered down the front steps. "Anthea!" he thundered. "And Calandra. Good God, even young Seabrook! Does your father know you are here, Weylin?" he demanded.

"Of course he does!" Weylin snorted before he could stop himself. Then hastily he said, "That is, good day, Mr. Marwood."

"I shouldn't think Mr. Marwood is in a mood to agree," Lord Radbourne observed dryly.

"And who the devil may you be?" Marwood demanded, looking up at his lordship.

Giles managed to execute the briefest of bows, without disturbing his horse. "I am Viscount Giles Radbourne," he replied politely. "And I collect you are Castor Marwood. Anthea's brother," some devil prompted him to add.

Marwood quivered with rage. "Radbourne? I've heard of you! How comes it about, sister, that this . . . this libertine has the freedom of your name? Have you actually had the impropriety to encourage the attentions of a man of his reputation? Before you answer me, Anthea, I take leave to warn you that Miss Lawley has already informed me that you have had Radbourne to tea!"

This last was pronounced in such awful tones that Anthea could not help laughing. "Yes, I have had him to tea," she agreed. "A high crime, I collect?"

"Don't be sarcastic with me, sister," Castor warned her imperiously. "I asked you if you have been encouraging this man's attentions."

Anthea did not answer at once. Instead, she signalled to Calandra to dismount. She further ignored Marwood's raging countenance while she gave instructions to the groom, who had by this time appeared. Only after this did Anthea turn to her brother and reply evenly, "I do think we should continue this discussion indoors. Whatever your wishes, I do not choose to make my neighbors a present of our affairs."

"I am not moving one inch," her brother retorted, "until you answer me, Anthea!"

"As you choose," she said evenly. "I, however, am going inside. Thank you, Giles and Weylin, for a most pleasant ride!"

With that, she simply started up the steps, oblivious of the furor she had left behind. Calandra hastily made her farewells and followed her aunt inside. Weylin was too surprised to speak and Castor Marwood was too angry. It was therefore left to Lord Radbourne to say, in a voice that could not conceal his amusement, "Come along, Seabrook. We don't wish to intrude further. A word of advice, Marwood. Your sister is not the sort of woman easily broken to bridle, and I shouldn't attempt it if I were you."

Stiff with outrage, Castor Marwood turned his back upon the pair and mounted the steps. An extremely interested Jeffries held the door and impassively informed Mr. Marwood that he would find the ladies in the drawing room.

Jeffries was correct. There Marwood discovered Miss Lawley tearfully trying to explain matters to Anthea. "I felt it could not possibly be improper to tell your dear brother, Mr. Marwood!" the poor lady said. "I am sure he cannot be blamed for feeling a most proper concern for you."

Miss Marwood spoke quietly but to the point. "Agatha, let me make this very plain to you. If I ever again find that you have been discussing my affairs with anyone, you leave this house! Proper or improper, I will not tolerate it. Do you understand?"

"Of course, my dearest Anthea," Miss Lawley replied with a distinct sniff. "I should never have done so if I had had the least notion you would object!"

Anthea doubted that, but she only said, "Very

well, that will be all for now, Agatha. You may go upstairs."

With a nervous flutter of her hands, Agatha Lawley retreated. Castor had, while watching this scene, had time to realise the unwisdom of his earlier approach. "Well, my dear, how are you enjoying Bath?" he asked his daughter affably.

Both ladies blinked at this abrupt change of both subject and mood. Not one to spurn such an overture, however, Cal replied, "Oh, tolerably well, Papa."

He nodded. "Acquiring a bit of polish, are you? Well, I daresay that's all to the good. I don't deny, however, that you gave us an anxious, a very anxious moment! Your Mama was quite upset to find you gone. Particularly when she had gone to such pains to bring a gentleman home to meet you, too. Now, was that kind?"

"I would scarcely call Lord Sterne a gentleman," Anthea said dryly.

"His birth is perfectly respectable," Castor replied.

"I was not speaking of his legitimacy!" Anthea retorted with some asperity. "Good God, Castor! You know the man's reputation as well as I do. Whatever respectability Lord Sterne acquired at birth, he has managed to lose along the way."

Stung by an accusation he could not refute, Marwood countered, "And what of Viscount Radbourne? I suppose you believe *his* reputation to be spotless? Perhaps you think he has taken a vow of celibacy?"

A chuckle escaped her. "Scarcely! Indeed, I *know* he has not!"

"*Anthea!*" Castor's eyes seemed to start from their sockets. "What are you saying?" he asked in failing tones.

Miss Marwood laughed again, but this time there was more than a hint of annoyance in her voice. "Must you be such a fool, Castor?" she demanded. "Your conclusion is scarcely flattering to me, but I suppose there is nothing new in that." She hesitated, then went on, "All I meant was that I have seen Lord Radbourne in company with a woman who was most certainly his mistress. And let me point out that one difference between Lord Sterne and Lord Radbourne is that Radbourne's tastes, at least, run to women who are old enough to come to his bed of their own free will!"

"How dare you speak like this to me?" Castor asked angrily. "In front of my own daughter, as well? God knows I had hoped you had outgrown this ... this eccentricity of character, but I begin to despair that you ever will!"

"It is not your affair," Anthea told him bluntly.

"Perhaps not," he replied, controlling his temper with great effort. "But it is my affair to whom you expose my daughter. Unless you give me your solemn promise, Anthea, that you will not expose Calandra to Radbourne's company, I must instantly remove her from your care!"

Miss Marwood turned away from her brother, a sudden constriction about her throat. How ... how absurd to be distressed about someone she had scarcely met ... barely begun to know! And yet Anthea found herself saying, "That will be ... be difficult. If his lordship remains in Bath, Calandra is bound to meet him. Unless you ...

you intend that I should keep her clapped up at home?"

Castor studied the back of his sister's head. Why the devil couldn't she look at him? Judiciously he said, "Well, that's true enough, and I don't mean that you should. Very well, I'll agree to accept your promise that Cal will only meet his lordship in public. That is to say," he explained sternly, "that there will be no threesomes or foursomes involving Radbourne such as I saw today. You will not invite him to dine here, or take tea with you, or indeed to attend any parties you might give while Calandra is with you. And in public she is not to speak with him unless it absolutely cannot be avoided. Do you agree to that?"

Quietly Anthea replied, "Very well, Castor. I promise that as far as it is in my power to do so, I shall see that Calandra does not meet Lord Radbourne."

"That's not fair!"

Anthea looked at her niece and spoke before her brother could. "Fair or not, if you wish to stay with me, that is how it must be. Your father does indeed have the right to say so."

The girl didn't answer, and Castor Marwood said uneasily, "Well, I still don't know, Anthea. Calandra, your Mama told me to bring you home, you know."

Anthea put a warning hand on her niece's shoulder. "My dear brother," she said evenly, "you may tell Eugenia that if Lord Sterne wishes to see Calandra, he may see her here. You may also tell Eugenia that if Calandra remains in my care, I will undertake to dower her."

Castor barely hesitated. Eugenia would be angry, to say nothing of Lord Sterne! But with five daughters to provide for, he judged Eugenia would come about quickly enough once she heard Anthea's offer. Aloud he replied, "All right. But mind you, Radbourne is not to come near my daughter—insofar as you can prevent it, Anthea. And now I should like my luncheon!"

6

Viscount Radbourne returned to York House, not in the least disturbed by what had occurred. To be sure, Marwood was an insulting, impertinent fellow. But Giles felt he knew Miss Marwood well enough to be certain that such intolerable interference in her life would only make her more determined to seek his company. Had she not called him "Giles"?

A smile played about Radbourne's mouth as he entered York House. How, he wondered, would Miss Marwood greet him the next time they met? With a sigh, he acknowledged that he would once more, no doubt, be relegated to the status of "Lord Radbourne."

At the door of his suite, Giles abruptly halted. Someone was waiting for him. Maggie. Carefully Giles closed the door behind him and patiently waited for her explanation.

"Don't be angry," she said coaxingly. "And certainly not at your valet. I told him you wouldn't mind if he let me wait for you here."

"You were mistaken," Radbourne said coldly. "I do mind."

Maggie raised her eyebrows in suprise. Then, without the least show of haste, she rose to her feet and approached the viscount. "Indeed?" she murmured. "I suppose you would have preferred a scene in one of the public rooms, where anyone might have seen us?"

Maggie came to a halt scant inches away from Radbourne's chest and tilted up her face to raise eyes that sparkled with unshed tears. Her breasts rose and fell visibly beneath the fabric of her dress, and the faintest scent of lilies reached his nostrils. A few weeks ago Giles would have swept her up into his arms and buried his face in her hair and branded her with his kisses. Instead, Radbourne smiled and said languidly, "You know, my dear, that I have the greatest dislike of scenes anywhere. Spare me, I beg of you, these theatrics. I told you in London that we were through. I have not, I believe, been ungenerous, and I am well aware that there are any number of gentlemen eager to take you under their wing."

Slowly Maggie lowered her eyes, and Giles had to admit that she did so with consummate grace. Her voice, when it came, was so low he almost had to strain to hear it. "I . . . I know that is what you told me," she said diffidently. "And I meant to let you go, but you must understand that I could not!" Once more her eyes met his, pleading eloquently as she went on, "I love you, Giles! I know that's not fashionable. I ought to have accepted your attentions, engaged in a light-hearted affair, then let you go without tears!

That was our bargain at the outset, was it not? I made you so many fine promises about how you need not fear I should try to entangle you! I swore I should no more expect you to be faithful than I would expect to stay young forever. So many promises, and yet now I find I cannot keep them. I have no wish to burden you, but I must know—is there any hope for us? For me?"

"None," he told her shortly.

In a swirl of skirts Maggie turned away from the viscount and strode to the far side of the room. There, her back against a window ledge, she faced him and said, "You're very cold-blooded, my lord!" Radbourne bowed and Maggie went on, her voice a sneer, "Why? What have I done, or not done, to you? I've always been there, always been available when you wanted me! Usually, anyway. And I never asked for explanations when you weren't. And for what? To be coldly thrust aside for a whim? That's what this is, isn't it? A whim? Some lady you caught a glimpse of in an inn, and you go off after her? My God, if I didn't know better, I might say you were in your dotage! Can you tell me even one thing she has to offer that I do not?"

Radbourne leaned against the wall, his arms crossed upon his chest. "Breeding," he answered succinctly.

Maggie's eyes flashed. "Breeding?" She laughed harshly. "I had no notion, my lord, you were such a worshipper at the altar of respectability! I felicitate you and wish you joy of the lady's breeding! Will you hug that word to you when you find yourself alone in bed because the lady is too well-bred to show the least bit of passion?"

As Radbourne's hand struck her cheek, Maggie's shrill voice fell silent. It was impossible to say which of the two was more astonished or more appalled at his action. "Get out of here," Radbourne told her in a dangerously quiet voice.

Maggie swallowed and nodded. She picked up her reticule from a chair and walked across the room. She hesitated by the door. "The York House is above my touch," she said quietly, "but if you want to find me, I shall be at the White Hart. For several days at least. If I must find another protector, I may as well try here in Bath."

Then she left. Giles waited until the door had closed behind her and then he turned and stared out of the window. I've never struck a woman before, he told himself, rather stunned. And I hope I shall never do so again!

You won't, another part of his mind answered dryly. You'll take good care not to allow any female to offer you such provocation.

Radbourne nodded curtly. He most certainly would not! And now, where the devil was his valet? Hiding, no doubt. He would know very well that he ought not to have let Mrs. Taggert in. The only thing that preserved Foster from the viscount's wrath was Radbourne's knowledge of just how persuasive Maggie could be. He didn't really blame the fellow, but that wouldn't prevent Giles from giving Foster a rare dressing-down. Lord Radbourne wanted to be very sure such a thing didn't happen again. Nor did Foster resent his master's lecture. He had been with the viscount far too long to overrate his lordship's anger. Aye, the master would come about soon enough! Particularly if his lordship was successful-like with this lady they'd come to Bath to see. And why shouldn't his lordship be? Wasn't a woman alive could resist him when he meant to win her over! Aye, he'd made a mistake, letting Mrs. Taggert in, but how was he to know matters had undergone such a change? His lordship had threatened to leave her before! Oh, but he'd give a great deal, Foster would, to see this lady that could make his lordship mean it. Quite out of the common way, *that* was a safe wager.

Anthea might have been out of the common way, but she was certainly not at her best as the day wore on. She had never realised before just how much she disliked her brother Castor and the way Agatha approved his every word. As most of Marwood's pronouncements were strictures on Thea's behaviour, it is scarcely surprising that her temper rapidly wore thin. When Castor finally retired for bed that night, sometime after Calandra had done so, Anthea rounded on her companion. "Really, Agatha! *Must* you toad-eat my brother so?"

"*Toad-eat?*" Miss Lawley was appalled. "Wherever do you get your expressions, my dear! And I am sure I have never done such a thing to anyone! When your brother speaks with such undeniable good sense, however, I feel it only right to applaud his wisdom."

"Good sense? Wisdom?" Anthea exploded. "And what, pray tell me, do you know of wisdom?"

"Why ... why, nothing, dearest Anthea," Agatha said, much taken aback. "And that is precisely my point! As mere females, we can scarcely expect to set ourselves up against your dear brother. I am sure he must know, far better than we can, what is best for us to do."

Miss Agatha Lawley was so evidently in earnest that the rebuke faded on Anthea's lips and she merely shook her head instead. It was scarcely the poor woman's fault if she believed what she said. No doubt she had been told it over and over again by her mother as she was growing up. It was therefore quite mildly that Anthea replied, "Well, you may treasure my brother's wisdom as much as you choose, just so long as you do not expect me to follow it."

Agatha, perceiving at a glance that her dear Miss Marwood had the headache, wisely changed the subject. "Will you be going to the Pump Room in the morning?" she asked brightly.

Anthea nodded. "You must know it is my brother's custom, whenever he chances to visit Bath, to nerve himself to drink the waters. He is convinced that they are beneficial to his health."

"Why, so they must be," Agatha agreed. "Everyone says so. Shall I come with you? To look after Miss Calandra? Then you may have a comfortable time with Mr. Marwood and not worry about the child."

The vision these words conjured up was so hideous to Anthea that she barely managed to repress a shudder. "I don't think that will be necessary, Agatha, but thank you for the thought," she said kindly.

"Now, don't thank me," Agatha said reprovingly. "Why, a fine thing it would be if I didn't contrive to make myself useful! Why, that's what I'm here for."

There could be no answer to that, and Anthea

was grateful that Agatha chose this moment to retire herself. Usually Agatha conceived it her duty to stay up as long as Anthea did so and see to it that all the candles were snuffed out, doors bolted, and so forth. In general, Anthea simply ignored such irritations, but tonight she was grateful that she did not have to. As Agatha had perceived, Anthea had the headache.

She had given her promise to Castor not to allow Lord Radbourne in her house. But as the hours passed, Anthea had begun to realise just how difficult a promise that would be for her to keep. And now, alone for the evening, she needed to think. She was no closer to any solution, however, when she sought her bed than she had been at the first. Sleep was elusive and, when it finally came, full of terrifying dreams.

7

Castor Marwood, his daughter Calandra, and his sister Anthea set out the next morning for the Pump Room. It was one of Castor's maxims that one ought never to delay a disagreeable task, and as he had managed to convince himself that drinking the waters was the only reason for his visit to this centre of Bath social life, he tolerated no delay. Marwood was, in fact, in excellent spirits, and in the glow of his enthusiasm, Anthea's quiet passed unremarked. "You look lovely, my dears," he observed graciously. "I must say, Calandra, that whatever else your aunt and I may cross swords over, no one can doubt she has excellent taste. I had no notion you were becoming such a beauty!"

Both ladies refrained from pointing out that this was a remark which scarcely reflected well on Mr. Marwood. Instead, they were content to allow him to carry on with his flow of good-humoured chatter. There was a shared, though unspoken hope that the better Mr. Marwood's mood, the sooner he might leave Bath and the likelier he would be to persuade Eugenia to agree to Anthea's custody of Calandra. For neither Miss Marwood doubted that the decision rested in that redoubtable woman's hands.

Their arrival at the Pump Room a short time later caused a minor flurry among the residents already gathered there. Since it was Castor's inevitable habit to visit whenever he chanced to be in Bath, he was well known to many of them. Indeed, among the retired military gentlemen, Castor Marwood was quite a favourite. One or two of Anthea's hopeful suitors, moreover, saw his presence as an opportunity to engage the entire party in conversation—an opportunity not to be overlooked, as Miss Anthea Marwood could be unaccountably difficult to approach when she was on her own.

Calandra, of course, was heartily bored by all of this, though her manners were too good to permit her to say so. Nevertheless, Anthea took pity on her niece and soon contrived to settle Cal with Mrs. Letty Balder and her daughter Melanie. In the short week Cal had been in Bath, she and Melanie had struck up a firm friendship. And as both Letty and her daughter were kind-hearted women, Calandra found herself basking in more warmth and approval than she had ever been accustomed to having. So Calandra was perfectly willing to sit with Melanie and her mother. Nor did Castor object. Mrs. Balder appeared to be a respectable, quiet woman and her daughter a most biddable girl. It would do Calandra no harm to be set such an excellent example! That Melanie's dutifulness was a deserved outgrowth of excellent parenting rather than a matter of principle never, of course, crossed Marwood's mind.

Meanwhile Francis Tanton was one of those who seized the opportunity to join Castor and his sister. "Your servant, Marwood," he said with a very precise bow. "Ma'am. May I say you are looking very lovely this morning, Miss Marwood? No doubt it is due to your very natural pleasure in having the company of your brother!"

"Thank ... thank you," Anthea said rather faintly.

This was a trifle too much, however, even for Castor, and he said severely, "There is no need to pay her such excessive compliments, Tanton. Always speak the truth, that's what I always say! Keeps a woman in her place."

Affronted, Tanton drew himself up taller. "I was speaking to Miss Marwood, and I shall say what I wish," he told Castor coldly.

With marked approval in her voice, Anthea observed, "Why, Mr. Tanton, I had no notion you had such a strong backbone!"

Before Francis could answer, he was forestalled by Castor exclaiming, "Good God, stop them, Anthea!"

It took Miss Marwood only a moment to real-ise what her brother meant. While they were talking, Lord Radbourne had arrived with Weylin. Giles was, in fact, bending over Calandra's hand as Melanie regarded his lordship with some-thing akin to awe and Letty appeared at a loss as to what to do. Anthea's voice broke into this charming tableau like a bucket of icy cold water. "Calandra, it is time we were going!"

Calandra looked at her aunt warily, then at Weylin. He moved closer to her side as Radbourne said warmly. "Good morning, Miss Marwood. How delighted I am to see you!"

Anrthea kept her eyes on the ground, for she knew that in spite of her promise to Castor, she would betray herself if she looked at Giles. "Good day, sir," she said as coldly as she was able. "Calandra, I said it was time to be going."

Sensing something amiss, Letty intervened quickly. "Please let her stay a little longer, Thea. If Mr. Marwood wishes to leave the Pump Room, well, I promise to return Calandra to you quite safely, later on."

Anthea shook her head. Cal, who had been whispering with Weylin, looked at her aunt in mute protest. Once again, it was Radbourne who spoke first. "Because of me, Miss Marwood?" he asked politely. At her nod, he turned and said to Calandra, "Obviously your aunt, my dear, does not wish to see you exposed to my company. I am at a loss to understand her enmity, but I am sure she will be only too happy to explain her reasons to you!" Giles paused and looked at Anthea. She did not speak, however, and he went on, pain evident in his voice, "Since it is my presence that is the problem, I shall withdraw, and then perhaps, Miss Calandra, you will be allowed to continue your tête-à-tête with your pretty friend."

So saying, the viscount bowed and strolled without haste from the room. No one, seeing his mild expression, could have guessed the rage he felt. No one except Anthea. Her own face was held so taut that Letty forbore to ask any questions. Weylin was not so perceptive. "That was a dashed rum way to treat him!" he protested hotly. "You might at least have told him what was wrong!"

Castor Marwood had joined the group just in time to hear this. "Young man," he said sternly, "that is none of your affair. I consider my sister to have acted most properly. If his lordship chances to be offended, all the better. He will be less likely to approach my sister or my daughter again."

For a moment it looked as though Weylin would speak, but he had been too well brought up to say what was on his mind, and so he bowed instead and walked away. Marwood watched him go, then turned to Anthea and said with a frown, "He is not, I hope, here making a cake of himself over Calandra? I should never countenance that match, you know."

Rather to everyone's surprise, it was Cal who answered. "Neither should I," she said. "However, as Weylin hasn't the slightest such interest in me, there is no question of such a thing."

Marwood snorted, but Anthea said slowly, "She's right, Castor. I did think, at first, he had a *tendre* for Cal. But now . . . well, I think he feels a responsibility toward her, and friendship, of course."

"Very well," Castor answered heavily. "But remember, Anthea! I hold you to account for my daughter's welfare!"

At this point, Letty intervened. With the gentlest of hints and very much to the relief of the rest of the party, Mrs. Balder contrived to send Marwood to the other end of the Pump Room in search of a mutual acquaintance. The ladies then settled back for a comfortable discussion. Anthea's composure, however, was shattered almost immediately as Calandra asked with a sigh, "I wonder where Lord Radbourne has gone?"

It was a question Maggie Taggert could have answered quite easily. Viscount Radbourne left the Pump Room in a rage. Anthea Marwood's actions were—must have been!—prompted by that idiot Castor Marwood! But that made the matter no better. Worse, in fact! Giles had not thought Miss Marwood the helpless sort of female to blindly obey anyone's commands, least of all her brother's! Nor had Radbourne missed the agony evident in her eyes. She wanted to see him, speak to him, and yet she had let herself refuse even to exchange the briefest of pleasantries with him. How dare she be such a coward?

It was in this foul mood that Giles arrived at the White Hart. Mrs. Taggert? Why, yes, she was here. He wished to see her? A servant would instantly be sent up with the gentleman's card, if he cared to leave it. The lady would no doubt descend to greet him. One must understand the White Hart's responsibility to protect its guests. The viscount bowed, extended his card, then took a seat. He did not have long to wait. The boy who had taken up the viscount's card soon returned with a note. Radbourne gave the boy a coin and unfolded the brief missive. It was evident that Maggie had written in haste, and the note merely gave directions to her room. Trust Maggie to see to it that no servant need escort his lordship! Giles waited a few moments, then strolled toward the stairs without haste. His rage, by now, had almost burned itself out, but not his determination to show Miss Marwood that there were other ladies who would not dream of spurning his attentions.

When Giles tapped on Maggie's door, it was immediately opened by her maid. As the woman took his hat and gloves, she contrived to indicate with the nod of her head that the viscount should go right on into the bedroom. There he found Maggie seated before her dressing table, a silver-blue wrapper half off her shoulders. Languidly she said, "Oh, hullo, Giles. You are up and about early, aren't you? Forgive me for not being dressed, but I was certain you wouldn't mind." Radbourne merely nodded politely. Maggie shrugged and said a trifle petulantly, "Well? Are you going to tell me why you're here? Or did you just come to stare?"

This last was spoken provocatively. Giles smiled and approached Mrs. Taggert, a slight swagger in his step. "Scarcely!" was his reply as he set his hands on her shoulders and planted a kiss on her neck.

A moment later she was in his arms, her hands exploring his body hungrily. His hands slid under her elegant wrapper, caressing the breasts and hips he knew so well. Impatiently Maggie's fingers tugged at the viscount's neck cloth, and she might have ripped open his shirt had Giles not placed a restraining hand over hers. "Careful!" he warned her with a husky laugh. "Both of us will find our reputations in shreds if I cannot contrive a creditable appearance when I leave here! Improvident of me, I know, but I did not think to bring an extra shirt along. As it is, my man Foster will cry when he sees the state of my neck cloth!"

Maggie laughed, a trifle breathlessly, and stepped back a pace. "Very well," she agreed. "You do it, then. Just don't take forever!"

And as the viscount watched, Maggie shed the last of her few garments and climbed into the nearby bed. Giles contrived to undress in little more time than it would have taken Maggie to do the job; then he too slid between the sheets, reaching eagerly for her. But Maggie was in a mood to play. She held him off with her hands and laughed as she said, "Not so fast, my lord! Lie still."

With an appreciative grin, Giles did as he was told, allowing Maggie to stroke her skillful hands over his face and chest and stomach. Then, when she came too close, he suddenly grabbed her and pulled her across him. Radbourne's hands were quite adept, and in a few moments Maggie was eager for *him*. Together they crested, and afterward Giles gently gathered Maggie into his arms.

But she would have none of it. Instead, Maggie sat upright and looked down at the viscount. "Well?" she said coolly. "Why have you come? Do you expect to go back to where we were before? Or is this in the nature of an accident? Perhaps you'll tell me you couldn't help yourself but that I'm not to expect it to happen again?" With a toss of her head, Maggie turned her back on the viscount. "Never mind," she said softly.

"I don't want to know if you're planning to go back to your fine lady."

"I'm not," he said shortly.

A gleam of triumph lit Maggie's eyes, but she was careful not to let the viscount see it. The face she turned to him was soft and hopeful, as was her voice. "Oh, Giles!"

Now Maggie let Giles hold her and soon had him eager for more of her womanhood. And before they were done, she had drawn from Radbourne the promise of an exceptionally fine emerald bracelet that she had seen in London. He was, moreover, to take her walking. If Maggie had her way, all of Bath would know the viscount was *her* property!

Giles had his own reasons for not objecting. Churlish though it might be, he hoped Anthea would see him with Maggie! So, in perfect accord, the pair soon dressed and Radbourne escorted Mrs. Taggert along the most-populated thoroughfares of Bath that he could discover. At one point they passed a jeweler's shop and Giles drew Maggie inside. There was, after all, the matter of the emeralds.

"I saw the very bracelet I want at Rundell and Rundell in London!" Maggie protested sharply when she realised what he was about.

"No doubt," Giles agreed. "But I am well aware, my dear, of how you dislike to be kept waiting for presents. And I've no notion when I shall be returning to London."

At this Maggie turned wide, angry eyes on the viscount. "I thought you said you were done with Miss Marwood!"

The jeweler perked up his ears at this mention of a name that was quite familiar to him. The viscount's next words, however, dashed his hopes of a juicy tidbit of gossip. "So I am, my dear. My acquaintance with Miss Marwood always was of the slightest degree, and now it is terminated altogether. Nevertheless, I feel no urgency in removing myself from Bath. And when I do go, I thought I might accept Calder's invitation to visit him in the shires."

There was nothing Mrs. Taggert could say to that, and after scarcely any further hesitation, she allowed herself to be persuaded to choose a bracelet. As the elegant trinket was placed on her wrist, Maggie reminded herself philosophically that a gift in one's possession was worth any number of promises.

Eventually they returned to the White Hart, where, to Lord Radbourne's delight, they encountered young Seabrook. "Hullo, Weylin," he greeted his friend affably. "I believe you've met Mrs. Taggert? Maggie, you recall Mr. Seabrook?"

Maggie nodded and extended her hand graciously. Oh, yes, she remembered the boy, all right! "How nice to see you again," she said in her warmest contralto voice.

"H-how n-nice to see you, ma'am," Weylin stammered.

Radbourne smiled to himself with a sort of vicious satisfaction. There was no doubt in his mind that Miss Anthea Marwood would be told of the encounter, and that was what he wished. Aloud he said firmly, "Upstairs with you, Maggie, my dear. I should like to talk with Seabrook."

"Will you be coming up later?" Maggie asked archly.

Radbourne hesitated. He had no wish to live in Maggie's pocket, not even to prove a point to Miss Marwood or her friends. "I think not. Tomorrow, perhaps," he replied coolly.

There was more than a hint of anger in Maggie's eyes as she snapped, "Good day, then, my lord!"

Weylin's eyes followed her as she left, and he was recalled to the present by Radbourne's dry observation, "In London they call her the Enchantress."

Weylin reddened and he said abruptly, "I had no notion she was here with you in Bath."

"With me?" The viscount's eyebrows rose. "She is here at the White Hart and I am staying at York House."

"You know very well what I mean!" Weylin persisted.

"Yes, I know what you mean," Radbourne agreed quietly. "But I cannot conceive what business it is of yours."

"I'm Miss Thea's friend!" Weylin retorted hotly.

Radbourne stared at Weylin, his attention arrested. In a puzzled voice he said, "Your championship of Miss Marwood seems to be misplaced, halfling. Or don't you recall the setdown she gave me in the Pump Room?"

"I do recall it," Weylin agreed evenly.

Radbourne continued to stare at Weylin. "And yet you're still angry with me," he said slowly. "I ask myself why, but confess I have no answer. In fact, I should have expected you to range yourself indignantly on *my* side of the snub she dealt me. It is distressing to discover my judgment of you to have been so mistaken."

"It wasn't mistaken!" Weylin blurted out.

Radbourne's eyebrows rose even higher at this, and the boy hastened to explain. "I ... I *was* indignant. I thought Miss Marwood should have told you why she wouldn't let you speak to Cal. But now I begin to think Mr. Marwood was right!"

The last few words were spoken bitterly as Weylin's eyes strayed toward the direction Mrs. Taggert had taken. Quietly Radbourne asked, "Why did Miss Marwood cut me?"

Weylin hesitated only a moment before he replied. "Because of Cal's father. He told Miss Thea that if she wanted Cal to stay with her, she would have to ensure that Cal had not the least acquaintance with you!"

The viscount considered this. "What about Anthea herself? Is she also to have nothing to do with me?"

Weylin shrugged. "I don't know."

Once more the viscount was pensive. After several minutes of silence he spoke. "Weylin, I should like you to do me a favour!"

A short time later, Giles sat in a hired hack outside Letitia Balder's lodgings. It was a new experience for him, waiting to see if someone would accept a visit from him. It was an experience he did not in the least enjoy. At last young Seabrook emerged and crossed over to the hack. "She'll see you," he said quietly.

"Thank you," Radbourne said. "And I shall see *you* another time."

Radbourne watched as Weylin set off on foot. He took a deep breath, alighted from the carriage, and paid the driver. Then resolutely he crossed the narrow street and rapped on Mrs. Balder's door. All too soon, it seemed to the viscount, he was bowing to Mrs. Balder as she looked him over appraisingly. "You are very good to see me," Radbourne said at last.

"Anthea Marwood is my very good friend," Letty Balder replied enigmatically. "Won't you be seated and tell me what this is about?"

"Thank you." Giles hesitated, then plunged on. "Perhaps you are aware that I have an ... an interest in Miss Marwood and that her brother, Castor Marwood, does not approve of the connection. Or so young Seabrook informs me. I had hoped your knowledge of the situation was more complete than his."

Letty Balder's eyes met Radbourne's and she spoke very deliberately. "Castor Marwood has given orders that so far as it is in her power to do so, Thea is to prevent any encounter between you and her niece. So far as I can discover, the ban is only on Calandra, and it occurs to me, my lord, that if you could contrive to encounter Anthea when she was *not* in the company of her niece, there could be no objection to that."

A tiny frown appeared between his eyes as Giles asked slowly, "Are you telling me that Miss Marwood wishes me to do so?"

Mrs. Balder hesitated. "I daresay your question comes of not knowing Thea very well. Anything of a deceptive nature is repugnant to her. If we could, however, present her with a *fait accompli*, I think Thea would not reject it."

"We?" Radbourne's eyebrows rose.

"Well, it did occur to me that Calandra and my daughter Melanie are becoming fast friends, and nothing could be simpler than for me to undertake to look after both girls in the mornings so that Thea might go riding as she is accustomed to do. And you might very easily encounter her when she does so."

"With a groom at her heels? I thank you, but no!" Giles said shortly.

Mrs. Balder placed a hand on his arm and said seriously, "No, but you don't understand! Thea long ago formed the habit of riding out alone. No one would think it unusual for her."

The viscount looked at Mrs. Balder's earnest face and asked, "Why are you doing this? Surely you know the reasons Marwood wishes to keep us apart. Why, then, do *you* find me acceptable?"

The words were spoken harshly, and Letty hesitated. Finally she said, "I detest round-aboutation, my lord, and much prefer pound dealings, so I'll tell you. Anthea Marwood is the best friend I have ever had and I would do anything I could to see her happy."

Radbourne was surprised into a harsh, cynical laugh. "And you think I am likely to bring it to her? Why not the opposite? Or *don't* you know my reputation?"

"I know it," Mrs. Balder replied tranquilly. "And I've brothers enough to know how much to believe of it! But I've also seen the way you look at Thea, and I cannot believe you would ever try to hurt her."

"I might do so without trying!" Radbourne snapped. "What then?"

"Anthea Marwood is not a piece of porcelain," Letty retorted dryly. "She won't break so easily. I'm more afraid she'll dwindle away, lost on the shelf, if you go away without seeing her again."

"Gammon! She has any number of suitors!" Giles answered with a wave of his hand. "I've seen some of 'em."

"Then you know that they are all extremely worthy gentlemen," she said coolly. When Giles nodded, puzzled, Letty went on, "Can you imagine Thea leg-shackled to any one of them? All cold propriety and impeccable breeding? *I* should have said that she would be better suited to someone with a different, warmer nature!"

In spite of himself, Giles laughed. "Very well," he said amiably. "Tell me when and where Miss Marwood goes out riding and I'll undertake to do the rest." He paused, then added almost unwillingly, "I cannot make you any promises, you know."

"I don't ask for any," Mrs. Balder replied calmly, "and neither would Thea."

They parted company a few minutes later, the best of friends. If either had any further qualms, they did not show it.

8

"Now, remember," Castor admonished his daughter, "you're to do everything your Aunt Thea tells you! If I hear you've caused her the least bit of trouble, home you come."

"Yes, Papa," Calandra said dutifully.

Castor nodded, satisfied. He then turned his attention to his sister. "I cannot say that I like this, Anthea, but so it is. I depend upon you to look after my Calandra, polish her up a bit, and keep her away from unsavory fellows!" He paused. "Do not be getting nonsensical notions yourself, my dear. You are, after all, thirty and may as well accept it. Though I suppose there are gentlemen, widowers perhaps, who are beyond the absurdities of romance and would welcome a mature woman to hold house for them. But it is the height of absurdity to expect such a thing from a man like Radbourne. Do not be mistaking a mere flirtation for anything more serious!"

Anthea, who had never been taught by her

family to rate her charms very highly, found nothing to cavil at in Castor's words. Had anyone told her that she was a lovely, desirable woman, Anthea would have been incredulous. "I am not a green girl," she assured her brother. "Nor need you have any fears about Calandra."

Castor hesitated. He stood with his sister and daughter on the steps beside his carriage. "I just don't know what Eugenia will say!" he protested plaintively.

"Just remind her that I am paying the bills for Calandra, and Eugenia will come about quickly enough," Anthea said soothingly. "Recollect that you've still the twins to provide for. And now you'd best be going," she added firmly. "I've no doubt Eugenia is anxious to see you!"

That was quite an understatement. Eugenia did not expect that Castor could reach Bath and return with Calandra in under four or five days, but that made the wait no easier. Mr. Oglesby, of course, was no problem. He was perfectly content to spend his days walking about the estate with Beatrice and her sisters. Or accompanying his fiancée on morning calls. Nor was he disposed to object to a quiet evening of cards or conversation. Lord Sterne, however, was not so easily satisfied. His first intention, upon learning of Marwood's sudden departure and Calandra Marwood's absence, was to depart himself. Eugenia Marwood was precisely the sort of illbred, mean-tempered, pinch-penny woman he abhorred. Nor was he enchanted by Beatrice Marwood or her worthy but very boring suitor, Mr. Oglesby. As for the twins, Drusilla and

Emeline, Sterne was only momentarily intrigued.
He was, it was true, partial to young girls, but
the twins were a trifle too immature even for
his taste. They were, moreover, inseparable, so
that the mildest of flirtations with either was
impossible. The only thing which kept Sterne at
Marwood's estate was his love of a scandal. And
something told Lord Sterne that Calandra Marwood's absence was both unexpected and irre-
gular, whatever Eugenia Marwood might say.

Still, Sterne was not prepared to wait more
than a week. After that, scandal or no, he would
leave unless Miss Calandra appeared. Though
even her arrival, he was inclined to believe, would
not suffice to keep him here. Indeed, having
seen the rest of Miss Marwood's family, Lord
Sterne asked himself what on earth had possessed
him to come to Marwood's estate at all! But he
was, he told himself, a fair man and he would
give the Marwoods a week to produce their
daughter.

Thus Eugenia Marwood was not the only one
to feel a sense of relief and expectation when
Winthrop entered the drawing room one evening to announce that the master had returned
home. Beatrice and Oglesby were too engrossed
in one another to much care, but Eugenia and
Lord Sterne were instantly on their feet. Particularly as Winthrop had given no indication of
whether Mr. Marwood had returned alone or in
company with his daughter. "I shall come and
greet him at once," Eugenia announced a trifle
shrilly. "Pray stay here and amuse yourselves,
all of you."

But Lord Sterne would have none of that.

"Oh, but I do beg you will allow me to accompany you and pay my respects to Marwood!" he said coolly.

Eugenia, though generally a most redoubtable woman, fluttered as she said, "Oh, no! That is ... there is no need, I am sure. Marwood will join you here as soon as he has put off his travelling gear. We have no wish to disturb you!"

Lord Sterne bowed. "But I insist, madam. I should not wish to be backward in showing any courtesy to mine host!"

There was nothing for it but to allow Sterne to have his way. Eugenia did so, devoutly praying that her capricious spouse had not failed her. They found Marwood leaving the foyer and headed in the direction of his library. Eugenia's peremptory tone brought him up short. "There you are, Marwood! Did you have a successful trip? Here is Lord Sterne to applaud your return."

Marwood, scarcely in the best of tempers to begin with, felt as though his neck cloth had suddenly grown too tight. "Hullo, my dear," he said, dutifully planting a kiss on his wife's cheek.

Lord Sterne, who had raised his quizzing glass, now said dryly, "It would seem Marwood's journey was *not* successful. Er, no doubt this is dreadfully *mal à droit* of me, Marwood, but where *is* your daughter?"

Unconsciously, Castor squared his shoulders and, avoiding his wife's sharp-set eyes, replied, "In Bath, my lord. Acquiring a bit of polish under the wing of my sister, Miss Anthea Marwood. Before her Season, you understand. Bringing her up to snuff before she makes her curtsey to the queen, don't you know."

"I see," Sterne said dryly. "Curiosity compels me to enquire if this means my suit is no longer welcome to her? Or rather I should say, welcome to you?"

Eugenia opened her mouth to reassure his lordship. Castor, however, had spent much of his journey home thinking about what Anthea had said. He had always stood somewhat in awe of his sister, whose intellect he considered to be too powerful by half, and he could not entirely dismiss her words. So now, to everyone's surprise, including his own, Marwood said bluntly, "You are, my lord! Very sorry to have dragged you here to no purpose. Never realised my Cal would take such a pet, but since she has, nothing to do but forget the whole business."

"Castor Marwood!" Eugenia said, fixing a fulminating gaze on her errant spouse. "Do you mean you have allowed *Calandra* to decide such a matter herself?"

Lord Sterne bowed at this point and spoke in a polite voice that dripped poison. "Please, madam, don't trouble yourself. I collect there is a young swain in Bath. Someone she prefers over myself? I only trust you will not have cause to regret her, er, impetuosity in *throwing* herself at the fellow!"

Goaded, Castor retorted, "Well, there you're out! There ain't no young swain. Leastways, Seabrook only escorted her and her aunt there. But he's dangling after someone else. If you must have it, my Cal's frightened of you! Aye, that's it. She's heard all manner of tales about you,

my lord. Good God, everyone has! And I tell
you, she's frightened."

Sterne, who had been listening with obvious
boredom, abruptly came alert. It was only with
great effort that he kept his voice steady as he
asked, "Did you say frightened?"

Castor, who by now had worked himself up to
a level of moral indignation, flung back at his
lordship, "Terrified!"

A smile briefly crossed Sterne's face as he
toyed with his quizzing glass. It was a sight
Eugenia Marwood greeted with no little relief.
Finally Sterne said, "Tell me, Marwood. If I
were to go to Bath and pay my addresses to
your daughter Calandra, would you object?"

"Of course not!" Eugenia replied hastily with
a minatory frown at her spouse.

But Castor scarcely saw her. "Do you mean
you still want to make my Cal an offer?" he
demanded incredulously.

"Well, as to that," Sterne replied smoothly, "I
can scarcely say until I've seen the child. At the
moment, I simply wish to assure myself that
you would have no objection."

"Too, too kind!" Eugenia murmured.

"Hmph!" Marwood snorted. "And I'd have
thought this would have given you a disgust of
the girl."

Sterne bowed slightly. "You mustn't blame
the child for her fears. Perfectly understandable,
I assure you. She has, after all, never met me. I
propose to remedy that."

Castor Marwood was still uneasy. His spouse,
however, had no intention of allowing mawkish
sentiments to interfere with the business of seeing

each of her daughters established creditably in marriage. Before Marwood could offer any further objections, Eugenia said, "We should be delighted to have you call on Calandra in Bath. I must warn you, however, that the child's aunt, Anthea Marwood, is . . . is rather out of the common way. An original, in fact! Sometimes I believe she has a dislike of men. In any event, you ought to be forewarned that she may not precisely welcome you, and I beg you will not regard such crotchets."

Lord Sterne replied easily, "I assure you, madam, that if I have *your* permission to pay my addresses to Miss Calandra, I shall scarcely be daunted by her eccentric aunt."

In perfect accord, the pair smiled at one another, and Castor said rather gruffly, "Yes, yes, by all means call on the chit. Just so long as you understand she's afraid of you. Haven't understood the girl in seventeen years, daresay I never will! Now, if you'll excuse me, my lord, I'm feeling devilish sharp set. Never can eat my mutton when I'm travelling. I shall see you in the morning. Eugenia, you'll make my excuses to Oglesby? Not that *he'll* care. Not when he can be making up to Beatrice, the sly puss. Smelling of April and May, they are. Leastways Oglesby is. Well, good night, all."

With that, Marwood made good his escape. In fact, however, Eugenia was not in the least inclined to try to stop him. Lord Sterne's pronounced intention to follow Calandra to Bath was as delightful as it was unexpected. She had no wish to find his lordship dissuaded by some careless utterance of Castor's. Eugenia, as she escorted Sterne back to the drawing room, attempted to repair any damage which might already have occurred. "I pray you will not regard it, Lord Sterne, if you find my daughter a . . . a trifle shy! It comes of not having brothers, you see. Calandra is, however, in general a most biddable girl and I daresay she will come round quickly enough once she has met you and seen that you are scarcely an ogre! Depend upon it, her aunt, Anthea, has stuffed her head with all sorts of nonsense. But you will no doubt make short shrift of that! Marwood and I have taken care to teach her her duty, of that you may be sure."

Eugenia might as well have spared her breath. Lord Sterne was not interested in discovering that Miss Calandra Marwood was a "biddable" girl. He hoped, in point of fact, that the chit was as frightened and reluctant as Marwood had said. If so, he could scarcely believe his good fortune. The parents who would countenance his attentions toward their daughters were very few. And in those rare cases, the daughters were, if not complacent, at least resigned to his suit. But Lord Sterne was bored by compliance. As the abbesses of several of London's most famous brothels could have attested, Sterne preferred his bedmates to be afraid of him. Afraid and young. Sterne's first wife had not been afraid. Fortunately she died in childbirth. The second had been as terrified as he could have wished, but she had found the means to hang herself before the marriage was scarcely twelve months old. Well, Sterne would take care to see that Miss Marwood took no such action! But first he must see this farce through and marry the chit, all right and tight. *If*, upon examination, she proved satisfactory.

None of these thoughts showed, however, on Sterne's face. Had Eugenia been asked, she would have said that she supposed his lordship to be slightly bored and that she could only hope that Calandra would not contrive to whistle him down the wind with her missish ways.

1

Meanwhile, Lord Radbourne and Mrs. Balder put their plan into effect. And so it was that three mornings after her brother had left, Anthea Marwood found herself riding alone toward the hills near Bath. It was a beautiful day and Thea was conscious of a sudden sense of freedom. She was very fond of her niece Calandra, but it could not be denied that the position of chaperon to a young girl had its drawbacks. Had Calandra been at her side, for example, Anthea would not have ridden her mare at a heedless gallop, as she fully intended to do as soon as she reached level ground. Not that Calandra was not an excellent horsewoman, but Anthea would not have allowed her charge to take the same risks that she took for herself. No, had Calandra been with her, Anthea would have insisted they enjoy a dull but respectable ride. For one had to begin as one meant to go on, and Thea fully intended to bring Calandra up to snuff before they went to London. What might be acceptable in Miss

Anthea Marwood, a respectable spinster, would not be countenanced in a green girl in her first Season. But it was very difficult to convince Calandra that it mattered!

So intent was Anthea on her own thoughts that she did not see the horseman until he spoke to her. "Good morning, Miss Marwood."

"Lord Radbourne!" Anthea exclaimed, unable to hide her pleasure at seeing him.

Encouraged, Giles brought his horse closer, his eyes taking in her blue riding-habit and flushed countenance. "I've missed you," he said quietly after a moment. "How do you go on?"

Radbourne's words abruptly recalled to Anthea her brother's orders, and she bent forward, pretending to pat her mare. With a careless shrug she said, "Well enough. And you?"

For a long moment Giles watched the back of Anthea's head before he answered rather dryly, "Not nearly as well as I should like. I know, by the way, about Marwood's orders."

Startled, Anthea was betrayed into looking at his lordship. "How can you? I mean . . ."

Giles moved even closer. So close that Thea was intolerably aware of how fine he looked in his riding coat and breeches. And then, before she could decide what to do, Radbourne had possessed himself of her hand. "I know that your brother wishes Calandra to be kept away from me," Giles said quietly, "but that need not keep us from meeting."

Anthea looked away. "Don't, my lord! You must see that it would not do!"

"Why not?" he asked. He waited until the force of his gaze caused Anthea to turn and meet his eyes. Then he went on, "If you tell me to go away—that you never wish to see me again—I shall. But be very sure, because I tell you frankly that I don't want to go. I understand your concern for your niece. If we continue to meet, it will assuredly be difficult. But what about your concern for yourself? Will you allow your niece's needs or your brother's orders to rule your life?"

Anthea withdrew her hand from Radbourne's grasp and said evenly, "I cannot see that I am making such a great sacrifice. If, at thirty, my heart has been untouched, I scarcely believe it ever will be. You've a *tendre* for me, and I confess I've one for you. But while I must be sorry for *you*, I cannot believe that someone with as cold a temperament as mine—"

"Fustian!" Giles cut her short rudely. "Don't try such farradiddles on me, girl! Cold temperament indeed! Shall I show you just how cold your temperament truly is?"

Without waiting for an answer, Giles reached out and drew Anthea Marwood very close to him. Before she knew what he was about, the viscount's lips had closed over hers: demanding, punishing, then softly pleading, stirring Anthea to her very soul. Frightened by the feelings she could not name, Anthea tried desperately to break free. After a moment, Giles let her. Shaken, she tried to steady herself and her horse. Grimly Radbourne watched her. "Well?" he demanded harshly. "Do you still persist in calling yourself *cold*?"

In spite of herself, Anthea smiled wryly. "I

scarcely think you would believe me if I said I did. My Lord Radbourne, I don't know—"

"I do!" Giles cut her short once more. "And I certainly hope you're not going to go into a decline simply because you've discovered you're a passionate woman!" he concluded acidly.

A gurgle of laughter escaped Anthea. She knew that her entire upbringing demanded that she deal his lordship a snub. Instead she said demurely, "Why? Don't you think I should make a lovely picture languishing away on the sofa in my drawing room?"

"My dear girl," Radbourne said through clenched teeth, "if I ever saw you *languishing* on a sofa, I would be strongly tempted to shake you, and I suspect that that is precisely what I would do!" Anthea laughed aloud and Giles nodded approvingly. "That's better. Come, our horses are getting restless."

"Very well," Anthea agreed. "My horse is in need of a gallop!"

And in the next instant, the very proper Miss Marwood most reprehensibly urged her mare to a neck-or-nothing pace. Radbourne passed her easily, but this time made no attempt to halt her horse. As she reined in at last, Anthea reflected that it was a wonderful thing to be with a man who would not be shocked by her need, now and again, to desperately break with convention! It was in that moment that Anthea decided that whatever Castor might say, she was not going to give up this newfound friend. Her face gave so little hint of her thoughts, however, that Radbourne asked, with some concern, "Are you tired? Shall we rest our horses and ourselves?"

Anthea nodded and indicated a nearby group of trees where they might tether the horses. Giles dismounted first, then turned to help Anthea. As his hands went round her waist, a thrill of warmth went through her. Then she was standing in the circle of his arms, looking up at him. After a moment, he let her go.

As Radbourne saw to the horses, Anthea tried to steady her confusion. It seemed scarcely any time at all before Giles put his hands on her shoulders and said from directly behind her, "Thea?"

Miss Marwood took a deep breath and turned to face Giles. His eyes probed her face for signs of distress and prompted a rather watery chuckle from Anthea. "You needn't worry," she said, tilting her chin up, "I *shan't* go into a decline over one kiss. But to put it plainly, I do find myself a stranger, at the moment. I had thought myself some sort of . . . of ice maiden, but now that notion is laid to rest."

"Good!" Giles said lightly. "I find I am not very fond of ice maidens, but I *do* like you."

Anthea smiled wryly. "That's all very well for you to say, but I must deal with the notion that I have quite sunk myself beneath reproach!"

"Is that how you see yourself?" Radbourne demanded impatiently. "What absurd fustian!"

Anthea smiled but shook her head. "To you, perhaps, but scarcely anyone else would agree. What oversets me most, you see, is the discovery that Castor may have been right—that I am unfit to have charge of Calandra."

Giles sighed heavily. "So you *do* regret kissing me."

Anthea hesitated only a moment. "I could fob you off with some sort of Banbury tale, but I won't. I regret nothing. Which only sinks my spirits further, you know, for I *ought* to regret it! The principles with which I was raised—"

"It is not my person that repels you, then?" Giles cut her short to demand. "It is the circumstances?" Anthea nodded, and he was the one to hesitate. At last he said lightly, "Well, then, surely the solution is a very simple one! Marry me and we may indulge ourselves in such conduct quite to our hearts' content and no one will be able to say you have sunk yourself beneath reproach."

With considerable constraint in her voice, Anthea replied, "Now you are roasting me, my lord."

"I am not!" he retorted firmly.

Anthea turned away, pacing the grass, clasping and unclasping her hands. "How can I marry you?" she demanded. "I scarcely know you! We should both regret it before a six-month was out!"

"I would take that risk," he answered quietly.

Miss Anthea Marwood paused and faced his lordship squarely. "I'm not sure that I would," she said seriously. "And in any event, you forget my brother, Castor. He would never give his consent to the match."

"You are scarcely underage," Giles pointed out calmly.

"He would take Cal away from me," Anthea replied. "And I cannot simply abandon her to be

forced into marriage with Lord Sterne. And . . .
and besides, I've no wish to be married!" she
concluded rather desperately.

For a long moment Radbourne regarded Miss
Marwood without speaking. Finally he possessed
himself of her hand and said quietly, "Very well,
dear heart! I've no wish to distress you. But
there are matters we must decide. Do you wish
to see me again?"

"Oh, yes!" There was no hesitation in Miss
Marwood's voice as she replied.

"Then we must decide how and where," Giles
said bluntly. "I believe we can contrive matters
so that your niece need not find herself thrust in
my company, but I warn you, Miss Marwood . . .
Anthea . . . that I do not intend to merely settle
for rides outside of Bath! I want to take you to
concerts and the theatre and I want to dance
with you at balls. So you'd best make your mind
up to it, my girl, and help me discover how we
may carry if off."

Miss Marwood bit her lower lip. "I must seem
such a dreadful wet-goose to you!" she said. He
nodded, and she added with some asperity,
"Well, you needn't agree so readily!"

In an exceedingly meek voice, Radbourne
replied, "My father told me never to contradict
a lady."

"Now, that is a shocking bouncer!" Anthea
told him severely. "Do give over such nonsense!"

"Certainly," Giles answered promptly, "If you
give over yours. Wet-goose, indeed! I haven't
known you very long, my dear, but long enough
to feel sure that you have your reasons for how
you feel. *I* may be impatient with them, but I

am certain they are no mere will-o'-the-wisps to you!"

Anthea smiled up at the viscount warmly. "You *do* understand, don't you? Perhaps another time I might even be able to explain. But not now."

As she spoke, Miss Marwood placed her hand on Lord Radbourne's arm. Without haste, so that she would have time to object if she chose, Giles took her in his arms again and kissed her. Anthea did not draw back, and when Giles did several minutes later, Miss Marwood rested her head on his shoulder. Lightly stroking her hair, Radbourne said, "Well, my dear? How shall we contrive to carry it off? Send Calandra to Mrs. Balder every morning?"

Instantly Anthea lifted her head. "How did you know that's where Cal is?" she demanded suspiciously. "Who told you?"

Giles stopped Anthea's questions by the simple expedient of kissing her. When he did speak, it was quite seriously. "Mrs. Balder is your very good friend. She told me about Marwood's objections to Cal being in my company. I asked her for help and she advised me to make a push to see you again. Mrs. Balder seemed to believe that I might make you happy. Was she so very wrong, then?"

Anthea wanted to deny it. But she could not, for she had always believed in pound dealings and she could not now bring herself to prevaricate. "No, she wasn't wrong." Anthea sighed. "I cannot send Cal to Letty's house every day, but when she does go, we may meet riding. Isn't that enough for now?"

"No." The single word was uncompromising.

Giles drew Anthea closer and said, "I want all of you and all of your time. I want the entire world to know that you're mine!" Giles paused, studied Anthea's face, then added with a sigh, "Very well. For now I shall settle for riding out with you. But I warn you, I shan't for long!"

Anthea smiled up at him and said warmly, "Thank you, my very dear friend!"

Determined to keep a light hand upon the reins, Giles released her and began to talk of other matters. Soon he had her laughing over the latest *on-dits* from London. Anthea countered with her own tales of Bath, and, to her delight, found that Giles shared all her amusement. *He* never once had to ask her what she meant or admonish her for a lack of either propriety or a respect for her elders. Indeed, as they rode back toward Bath much later that morning, Anthea told Giles, "Do you know, my lord, it is very strange, but I feel as if I have known you all my life."

Radbourne chuckled. "Thank God you have not! I doubt any romance could survive the knowledge that either of us had seen the other in short coats! Though I must say, I wish I had known you in your salad days. It seems intolerable to me that you have been on the shelf all these years."

Anthea coughed and said dryly, "Yes, well, my lord, as I recall, you were married the year of my comeout ball. It was the match of the Season and you scarcely had eyes for anyone except Clarissa Lambert. What a diamond of the first water she was! Every gentleman in London was after her hand, and you were considered quite the luckiest man in England to have won it." Anthea laughed without rancour. "She cast the rest of us into the shade and I don't mind telling you that we were all very grateful that *someone* took her out of the running and the gentlemen might once again notice the rest of us! And of course by the time you came out of mourning for her, I was already here in Bath with my mother." Anthea hesitated, then said, "Tell me more about Clarissa."

Radbourne's smile disappeared and when he spoke there was a great deal of constraint in his voice. "I've told you we were not happy. Clarissa . . . well, Clarissa discovered that marriage was rather tame after having been the toast of London. She hated the countryside—and London scarcely less, when she discovered herself deserted by all her former suitors. I thought perhaps that children would be the answer, but Clarissa was terrified of childbirth and determined, moreover, not to ruin her figure with breeding. So, within months of the wedding, she deserted my bed. And it didn't take her much longer to discover that recklessness drew her the attention she craved. By the time Clarissa died, thrown by a horse far too wild for her, she had long since ceased to think of me as anything save a source of the presents she loved and as a means to make other women jealous."

"How . . . how dreadful for you," Anthea said, feeling rather shaken.

Radbourne shrugged and answered roughly, "At least I had no fear that she would cuckold me. Clarssa was far too frightened of having a child to share any man's bed! She would accept—

and indeed sought—everything short of it, but I never needed to fear that." Giles paused, then said huskily, "Everyone—women, I mean—called Clarissa a heartless jade. Even pitied me. But I often wonder how much *I* was to blame. I made no effort to soothe her fears, but only mocked her for them. Nor did I show much patience on our wedding night. Or later. I wanted Clarissa too much. Nor had I any notion of considering her pleasure—I only thought of mine. Had I had more patience or better understood her needs, Clarissa might not have killed herself. Do you know, when I heard she was dead, my first thought was to feel relief? And yet I believed I loved her!"

The pain was sharp in Radbourne's voice, and Thea took a moment to answer. Finally she said slowly, "If you loved her, then your relief must, in part, have been for her. That such misery was finally over." Anthea closed her eyes a moment, then opened them and added quietly, "I felt much the same when my mother died. I cannot remember a time when my mother was not unhappy. All my life I had heard her talk of the things that frightened her or hurt her or left her raging with frustration. And I know that had she lived, the rest of her life would have been the same. And so, though I loved her, I too felt relief when she died."

"Is that why you're afraid of marriage?" Giles asked with a frown. "Because your mother was unhappy in hers?"

"In . . . in part," Anthea agreed.

"Perhaps that was because of what she brought to wedded life," Giles suggested gently.

Anthea looked down at her hands, and it was some time before she could answer. Her voice shook as she said, "I have my own reasons for knowing the marriage could not have been a happy one, whatever the circumstances! Though I grant you, even a saint would have had trouble pleasing my mother!" Anthea paused and realised Radbourne was about to speak. With a very real terror in her voice she cried, "No, no more questions, please!"

It was impossible for Giles not to be aware of how pale Anthea had gone. Or of the fact that she was still trembling. His own troubles forgotten, he hastened to reassure her. "I shan't press you," he said. "But please believe that if you ever wish to tell me, I shall be here to listen!"

Once more Anthea said warmly, "Thank you, my very dear friend!"

Giles exerted himself to put her at ease, and succeeded so well that, by the time they parted company on the outskirts of Bath, Anthea once more found herself able to laugh. It was, she thought, taking a deep breath, a *wonderful* day!

10

Anthea Marwood did not think the day so wonderful, later that afternoon. She and Calandra were in the drawing room, both attempting to compose dutiful letters to Castor Marwood. Agatha, aware of dear Anthea's preoccupation, was determined that nothing should disturb her. How fortunate that Miss Calandra was, for once, equally quiet, for the child, while delightful of course, was rather too lively. *Not* that Agatha would ever dream of saying so! No, she would just tiptoe about and rearrange the room just as dear Miss Marwood liked it. And when the knocker sounded at the door, Agatha was tempted to rush out and tell Jeffries to deny all callers. Only the comforting reflection that, at this hour, whoever it was must have mistaken the house, prevented her. It was a shock, therefore, when moments later Jeffries opened the drawing-room door and announced, "The Marquis of Sterne."

Agatha was in such a flutter over his lordship's title that she failed to notice how dreadfully pale Calandra had become or that dear Miss Marwood had pressed her lips tightly together in an angry line.

Miss Marwood did not, however, forget her manners. "Good afternoon, my lord," she said coolly. "Won't you sit down?"

Anthea was well aware that Calandra was looking at her in stunned reproach. But in the moments since his lordship had entered the room, Thea had taken Sterne's measure. To show the least sign of fear or distress would be fatal. Instead he must find her calm, composed, and simply bored by his pursuit of Calandra. If he could be so convinced, he might well abandon Cal for more intriguing game. It was with this in mind that Anthea commanded her niece, "Make your curtsey to Lord Sterne, Calandra, my dear."

Rebelliously Cal did so. In turn, the marquis bowed before taking a seat. "How utterly charming you are, my dear. Indeed, both of you are as delightful as I have been told! And this lady?"

"Miss Agatha Lawley, my companion," Anthea replied evenly. "Agatha, you may go."

Agatha had no choice but to withdraw. She could not suppress a flutter of excitement over the distinguishing attention the marquis had shown her. Nor could she entirely suppress her resentment at having been dismissed. Her dear friend Hetta would have so enjoyed hearing about the marquis' visit!

Anthea Marwood knew all about dear Hetta. That was one of the reasons she had sent Agatha out of the room. Anthea was aware that the news would soon be bandied about Bath that

Sterne had come in pursuit of Cal. But she was determined to have no witnesses to the setdown she intended to give the marquis. When she and Cal were alone with Sterne, Anthea said coolly, "You said that you had been told my niece and I were charming. May I ask where you came by such a notion?"

"Why, from your brother—Miss Calandra's father," Sterne said in apparent surprise. He wagged a playful finger at Thea as he added, "Marwood said I should find you a most careful guardian of Miss Calandra!"

"If you've been so warned," Anthea said dryly, "then I wonder that you have wasted your time by coming to Bath."

Sterne laughed heartily and said, "I wished to let Miss Calandra see that I am scarcely the ogre she apparently imagines me to be. I'm simply a man like other men! And while I should scarcely try to force the girl to the altar, I do wish she would bring herself to consider my suit."

"But you're not like other men!" Calandra retorted hotly. "Everyone says—"

"*Calandra!*" Anthea spoke sharply, silencing her niece.

Sterne inclined his head toward Thea. "Thank you, my dear lady. I should not like to think that my suit had been rejected merely because of what *everyone says*! The gossip is much exaggerated, I assure you. And I am persuaded, Miss Marwood, that you are far too sensible to allow the child to commit such a folly."

"*Folly?*" Cal gasped in outrage.

Anthea once more silenced her niece, this time

with a look. She then addressed his lordship. "Certainly there is no need to regard such gossip," Thea agreed affably. "And I believe you will find my niece is too well-bred and has too much common sense to do so."

"Why, thank you," Sterne murmured, highly gratified.

Anthea smiled at him then went on sweetly, "Indeed, I cannot think why my niece bothered to mention your reputation. After all, it is enough to point out the difference in age and experience between the two of you to realise that such a match is out of the question."

Sterne's smile disappeared and he said evenly, "My dear Miss Marwood, your brother and his wife do not agree. Just yesterday, in fact, he reaffirmed his support of my suit!"

Anthea listened politely, then said, "Ah, but you see, Lord Sterne, the only relevant question is whether Calandra wishes to hear your suit! Do you, my dear?"

"No!" Calandra fairly spat the word. "I don't care what my father told you—I won't ever marry you! I won't!"

Sterne rose, the last vestige of a smile completely gone from his face. "You shall," he said briefly. A moment later and the smile was back in place as Sterne bowed to Anthea. "What I mean is that I cannot accept that this irrational dislike of me will persist in the face of a better acquaintance between us. I shall remain in Bath so that your niece may have the opportunity to come to know me."

"You are wasting your time," Anthea told him frankly. "Here in Bath, Calandra is in my care, and I warn you that so long as she chooses not to see you, you will not be permitted to call on her."

Sterne waved a hand airily. "Unless the child chooses to shut herself up like a prisoner, we are bound to meet. And in any event, I find within myself a sudden desire to take the water here. So don't worry about me, my dear lady! I shall contrive. I *shall* contrive."

Then, with another bow, Sterne was gone, escorted to the door by an intensely curious Jeffries. How utterly daunting that Lawley had been sent from the room! Otherwise Jeffries could have looked forward to a comfortable cose with her and known what had set the ladies all atwitter. Ah, well. Perhaps the mistress would confide in Lawley later. One could always hope so.

But in the drawing room, neither Calandra nor her aunt had any intention of confiding in Agatha. "I won't see him again," Cal warned Thea.

"I'm not asking you to," she replied mildly. "You may be quite sure that Jeffries will have his orders to deny Lord Sterne in the future. But Sterne is correct, my dear," she added meditatively. "If he remains in Bath, you are bound to meet. I don't ask you to be more than civil to him, but anything less would lead to just the sort of gossip we wish to avoid."

"I don't care!" Cal retorted defiantly. "I shan't be civil to him!"

"Well, I do care," Anthea countered. "I am determined not to give Castor—your father—the least excuse to remove you from my care. So, we shall be polite to his lordship. Sooner or later he must grow tired of such a pointless pursuit of you!" It was evident to Anthea that her niece was unconvinced, and after a moment she went on, "You must give Sterne no reason to believe, Cal, that you are afraid of him. Perhaps I ought not to say this, but I believe Sterne to be a man who finds excitement in frightening young girls. The quickest way to dampen his ardour for you is to let him see that you are not the least bit afraid of him."

Calandra shuddered and answered very quietly, "I don't know how it is, Aunt Thea, but he *does* frighten me! Your advice is all very well, but he'll see that I'm afraid. You know I'm no good at cutting a sham!"

Anthea patted her niece's hand and said reassuringly, "Well, my dear, so long as I am around, I promise you, you've nothing to fear."

Calandra gratefully hugged her aunt. At that moment, Agatha entered the drawing room, still all aflutter. "Jeffries told me his lordship had gone. Such a gentleman! All proper attention to you and *so* distinguished-looking. How exciting Miss Calandra is to have *such* an ardent suitor!" she concluded playfully.

Cal was too well-bred to reply as she would have wished. It was left, therefore, to Anthea to say coldly, "That will do, Agatha. You know very well that Cal came here to escape Lord Sterne's unwelcome attentions. You may be able to overlook his age and reputation, but *we* cannot. You will oblige me by remembering that in the future, Agatha!"

Thoroughly cowed, Miss Lawley said, "Yes, Miss Marwood."

"Good. You may have the rest of the afternoon off."

Frightened now, Agatha hastily retreated. When she was gone, Calandra said thoughtfully, "I don't think she likes me, Aunt Thea."

"Who? Agatha?" Thea smiled wryly. "No, I don't suppose she does. Can you blame her? Think what it would be like to be an indigent female, unmarried, and dependent on the generosity of your relations! Or some stranger who has hired you to run errands for her. Dependent, you see, on the whims of a person who could turn you out at any time. Agatha sees you as a threat, I suspect. What if you should supplant her in my affections? Suppose you never married and instead made your home with me? I might dismiss her, and then where would she go? Even if she contrived to have saved enough to live on, she would be all alone. *Not* an enviable state for a woman, particularly a woman as timid as Agatha. Even I should not relish such a state!"

"But would you really do that to her?" Cal asked, rather awed at the notion.

Anthea smiled as she shook her head. "Of course not. If I ever dispense with Agatha's services, I should make certain she had another place to go to. But I've recounted to you *her* fears. And no amount of reassurance on my part is likely to remove them. So do try to understand if Agatha is rude to you."

Cal nodded. "I shall. How grateful I am, Aunt Thea, that I'm not likely to stand in her shoes someday! You know, I never thought how unpleasant it could be, not to marry. I always think of you and of how happy *you* seem to be."

A shadow crossed Miss Marwood's face, and there was constraint in her voice as she said, "Do you envy me, Cal? Don't, I pray you! My lot is a far more fortunate one than Agatha's, but even I feel a lack at times and wonder if this is all there shall ever be."

"Why haven't you married, then?" Calandra asked, genuinely puzzled. "I know you haven't lacked for suitors, and you've even liked some of them."

Anthea stared down at her hands. How strange to be asked the same question twice in one day! It was some time before she answered. "Because the only thing worse than being alone is an unhappy marriage!" she said quietly. Then she added, a trifle impatiently, "But I don't think that all marriages have to be unhappy! For God's sake, Cal, don't be ruled by *my* fears—or anyone else's! Keep your wits about you, and I don't doubt you'll find the right husband for you. Don't marry out of fear, but neither should you stay single out of some absurd notion that it is inherently a desirable state."

Impulsively Cal hugged her aunt again. "Dearest Aunt Thea! I only wish you would take your own advice."

Patting her niece's back, Anthea said wryly, "So do I, Cal. So do I. Now, go and finish your letter. *I* shall have to start over with mine, since I intend to tell Castor and Eugenia just what I think of their support of Sterne's suit!"

Cal giggled but dutifully turned to her writing desk. With a sigh she picked up her pen. A thought occurred to her and she said, "I wonder what Wey will say about all this. How fortunate he's coming to tea today!"

Weylin, when he arrived, however, had other matters on his mind. After greeting Calandra and Thea rather absentmindedly, he blurted out, "I've got to go back home. Papa is ill and Mama says he is asking for me."

"Poor Wey!" Calandra exclaimed.

"How ill is he?" Anthea asked quietly.

"I don't know," Weylin said, running a hand distractedly through his hair, "and that makes it particularly worrisome. Mama's letter was three pages long, but she crossed and recrossed her lines and blotched them with crying so that there is no getting any real sense out of them. I shall have to go home and see for myself. Don't you agree, ma'am?"

Anthea did. Particularly as Weylin's parents were sensible people who had never tried to keep him tied too close to home. If they said he was needed, then there could be no doubt that he was needed. So she assured Weylin that she understood and then asked, "When do you leave?"

"Now," he replied instantly. "I only came to tell you before I left. My things are already on their way, I've paid my shot at the inn, and my horse is outside and saddled waiting for me." He paused and turned to Calandra. "I'm sorry to desert you, Cal, but you really don't need me anymore, and I do have to go home. Please explain to Melanie for me, will you? Oh, and write and let me know how many hearts you break while I'm gone!"

Cal nodded and managed an uncertain smile. "Give my love to your parents."

"I shall," Weylin promised.

"And write to let us know how he goes on," Anthea added as he turned to take his leave of her.

A few minutes later, and Weylin was gone, sped on his way by the two ladies who stood watching on the steps until he was out of sight. Then slowly they went inside while Jeffries held the door for them. And that poor fellow was once more left to his own conjectures.

11

"Perry!" a delighted voice cried out.

Lord Sterne slowly turned, reluctant, it seemed, to discover just who was hailing him in the lobby of the White Hart. When he did see, he bowed slightly and spoke coolly. "Good day, Mrs. Taggert."

Maggie Taggert made a moue with her lips and laid one delicately gloved hand on his lordship's sleeve. "So formal?" she asked archly. "I thought we were friends?" Sterne merely bowed again, and Maggie laughed as she withdrew her hand from his arm. "Very well. So you've good cause to still be angry with me! Let us find a quiet corner where we may talk, and I shall undertake to be good."

For a moment it seemed that Sterne would refuse. But he did not. His lordship shrugged and said indifferently, "Very well. As you wish." To the efficient man at the desk he added, "You will see that that parcel is delivered directly, won't you?"

"Of course, my lord."

"Good. Very well, Mrs. Taggert, you shall lead the way. I am all patience today."

Maggie smoothed her skirt, avoiding his lordship's eyes as she asked mildly, "Whom was that parcel going to, Perry?"

"That, my dear, is none of your affair," Sterne replied, rather amused.

"It would not have been—by chance—for Miss Calandra Marwood, would it, *dear* Perry?" she said innocently.

"The devil!" Sterne was no longer amused. "How did you come to know of this?" he demanded.

Maggie studied his lordship a moment before she replied. "No need to rip up at me, Perry. I can keep my tongue between my teeth. *When* I choose to do so. And I shall, for now."

By now they had found that "quiet corner" and Sterne had recovered himself. "There scarcely seems any need for you to if the news has already gotten about that I'm dangling after the chit," Sterne said blandly. "Devil take it, though! I thought I had been discreet. No one but Marwood and myself knew I was coming to look over his daughter."

Maggie took pity on his lordship and explained, "Radbourne told me. He has, it seems, befriended Miss Marwood's aunt, and she told him. So you needn't fear to find your behaviour an *on-dit.* Yet."

Sterne's eyes narrowed as he studied Mrs. Taggert. "I see. And you are not pleased that Radbourne has, as you so delicately put it, befriended the aunt. But I confess that I fail to see

how that leads to your interest in the niece.
Unless Radbourne has turned his eyes in that
direction also?"

"Don't be absurd!" Maggie said angrily. Agi-
tated, she rose and paced about. "I don't care in
the least about the niece! It's the aunt I should
like to serve a backhanded turn. But I had no
notion how until I saw you."

Sterne spread his hands. "My dear Maggie, I
fail to see how *I* can help you. Unless you are
suggesting that I pursue the aunt? A lovely
creature, I agree, but you, of all people, must
know that my taste runs to younger morsels."

Maggie threw him a fulminating look. "I'm
scarcely likely to have forgotten," she said in a
withering tone. "You were, after all, quite explicit when you turned down my offer of an
affair."

"Then what do you expect of me?" his lordship asked.

Maggie's lips tightened. "I want you to succeed with the niece. Giles tells me the aunt is
very fond of her, and your suit distresses her a
great deal."

"Ah, but you would gain nothing more than a
trifling revenge," Sterne pointed out ingenuously.

Maggie paused in her pacing to slap a small
table with the palm of her hand. "I *want* revenge,
trifling or not! I should be delighted to discover
that someone—anyone except Giles—had become
betrothed to Miss Marwood. But lacking that, I
shall happily settle for revenge."

"Very well," Sterne agreed, "you would like
to see me succeed. Obviously I should prefer the

same thing. But I still fail to see why we are having this conversation."

Maggie looked at him squarely. "Because I intend to help you, Perry. I don't know how, yet, but I intend to help you. I *can* tell you that the girl is often seen in the company of a Mrs. Balder and her daughter. *Without* the aunt, upon occasion."

Sterne considered the matter judiciously. Finally he said, "It's a start. And I shan't deny, Maggie, that I would be grateful for your help. Instinct tells me Miss Calandra Marwood is terrified of me, and I am determined I shall bring her to bed!"

Maggie looked at him oddly. "I said I would help you, Perry, and I shall. But I confess that *I* don't understand your pursuit of the chit. Surely it would be simpler and perhaps safer to wed a chit less—shall we say—averse to your suit?"

Sterne smiled at her. "But you know how *stimulating* I find fear," he protested mildly.

"There are plenty of frightened girls to be bought in London," Maggie told him bluntly. "This one has a family. The *ton*, moreover, would not forgive you a scandal with one of their own."

Sterne's smile deepened. "Don't you see, my dear, that that only adds spice to the matter? This chit has spirit. I scarcely think she'll hang herself as the last one did. And I brushed through *that* scandal tolerably well, didn't I?" Reluctantly Maggie nodded, and Sterne went on, "You can't imagine my anticipation! This one will fight me—I know she will! What delight I shall have in subduing her!" In spite of herself, Maggie shuddered, causing Sterne to laugh. "Confess," he taunted her. "You're grateful now, aren't you, that I turned down your offer of an affair!"

"By God, yes!" Maggie flung back at him.

Sterne laughed again and warned her playfully, "Careful, my dear, or I may change my mind. Your offer is still open, I assume?"

Maggie paled. Lord Sterne rose and swaggered insolently toward Maggie, who seemed frozen in place. The closer he came, the paler she grew, until he stood a scant few inches away from her. Without the least haste, Sterne reached out and stroked her cheek. Maggie could not keep from flinching. "Giles won't like this," she warned him.

"Do you intend to tell him?" Sterne asked with mock surprise. Then his laugh was chilling as he said, "My dear Maggie, if I decide to take you, no one, including Radbourne will be able to stop me!" His hand strayed insolently lower to stroke the curve of her bosom as he went on, "Picture it, if you will, my dear. I should be sure to carry you off somewhere so isolated that no one would find or disturb us until it was *far* too late. But then you would be begging to stay with me." Still lower Sterne's insistent fingers strayed, stroking Maggie's thighs through the thin muslin of her overdress. When they reached the triangle between her legs, she gasped, triggering another laugh from Sterne. "You see?" he said. "Already you want to come to me. Shall I forget Calandra Marwood and take you instead?"

With another gasp, Maggie broke free. Her breath came quickly as she cried, "No! You don't want me! You said so, before. You . . . you prefer younger girls."

Sterne chuckled, and one of his hands ran up Maggie's neck. She flinched, and he said, "Ah, but that was before I knew how delightfully frightened *you* could be!"

As his hands reached for her again, Maggie backed away. All too soon she found herself trapped against the wall. "So," Sterne said mildly, "we find ourselves even. I have given you a fright to match the setdown you gave me in London. Don't worry, my dear Maggie. You are safe enough for the moment. In spite of your evident fear of me, my taste does still run to someone as young as Miss Calandra Marwood. I shall, however, avail myself of any help you may have to offer. But I warn you, my dear, not to change your mind and try to cross me on this. If you did, I should be forced, you see, to teach you a lesson. And even though I prefer younglings, I should avail myself of your charms— quite unflinchingly, I assure you. In spite of whatever protests you might try to make! And when you were utterly my slave, begging me to bed you, I should turn you out in the back streets, in your shift, I think, and watch as the jackals took their turn with you. As they would when they saw that I should reward rather than punish them for it. Do I make myself quite clear, Maggie, my dear?"

Unable to speak, she nodded, pressing herself still closer against the wall. Sterne laughed and stepped back to give himself the room to execute a bow. "Good. I shall see you later, then. Good day, Mrs. Taggert."

It was only some time after he had gone that Maggie's colour returned and her heart stopped racing. And even so, her knees felt so weak that she was obliged to sit down. Dear God! What was she going to do? It was, at that moment, Maggie's devout wish that she had not set eyes on Lord Sterne and that even if she had, that she had had the sense not to speak to him! Her first impulse was to flee to London. But there was Giles to be considered. She had worked too hard and too long to let him slip through her fingers now. He must, he would, come up to scratch! Maggie Taggert was determined that before the year was out, she would be Lady Margaret Radbourne.

Meanwhile, it would be interesting to know what had been in the parcel. Perry had evidently sent it to the Marwood girl. How provoking not to know for certain what was in it! Maggie fully intended to help Sterne, but she was equally determined, if it was at all possible, to acquire something, some sort of information perhaps, with which to protect herself in the event that something went wrong!

12

That same parcel caused a certain degree of consternation in Miss Marwood's household. It held a cunningly wrought brooch set with tiny amethysts and sapphires. Rather in awe, Calandra told her aunt, "I wonder who could have sent it."

"Is there no card or message?" Anthea asked.

"No, none. And I particularly looked for one. I thought at first that it might have been Wey, but he isn't in Bath any longer."

"It doesn't really sound like him, anyway," Anthea observed judiciously. "Who else could it have been? Pitney, perhaps?"

"That's it!" Calandra gave a cry of delight. Then, blushing, she hesitated and tried to say with dignity, "He ... he has been rather ... rather attentive of late. I ... I rather think he likes me. Would you object if he did?" she asked her aunt.

Anthea shook her head, with a smile. "Recollect that I am not your guardian," she warned her

129

niece, "however much we may wish I were. But, no, I can see no reason to object to Pitney."

In answer, Cal hugged Anthea. "Dearest of aunts!" she said. Then she spoke diffidently. "The brooch, it's rather a dear piece, isn't it? Ought I to return it, do you think? Would it seem too particular if I accepted it?"

Anthea replied dryly, "Since this is entirely conjecture and we do not know for certain who sent you the gift, I don't see how you can return it. No, I think it would be unexceptionable for you to accept it. You can always return it later, if you discover your admirer's identity and feel it wiser to do so."

Calandra nodded. "You have an answer for everything, don't you, Aunt Thea?"

She laughed. "I only wish I did, my dear!"

At that moment Miss Lawley entered the drawing room and immediately caught sight of the brooch and the box it had come in. "What a darling gift!" Agatha tittered, and wagged a finger at Calandra. "From a persistent suitor, no doubt. I wonder who it can be."

Calandra cast a helpless look at Anthea, who immediately said in firm tone, "It's time for you to go upstairs and change, Calandra. You are due to go out with Mrs. Balder and Melanie, and I am expecting my horse to be brought round any minute."

"What? Riding in the afternoon?" Agatha exclaimed. "You will not! My dearest Papa was used to say that the afternoon sun was far too hot for riding. You will surely wait until morning for such an exercise."

Anthea smiled perfunctorily. "I am going riding *now*, Agatha. Come, Cal. We'd both best hurry."

Hastily the younger Miss Marwood gathered up brooch, box, and silver paper that had wrapped it. "*I* think it's marvellous that you're going riding now," she told her aunt sweetly. "Perhaps I ought to come with you."

As Miss Lawley stiffened with outrage, Anthea laughed and tapped her niece's cheek. "Doing it much too brown, Cal! As if you would really prefer my company to Melanie's! *Particularly* as I understand there are two or three young gentlemen to accompany the three of you to the park."

Calandra laughed, and in perfect accord, the two Misses Marwood went upstairs to change. A short three-quarters of an hour later, Anthea was galloping toward a copse of trees outside of Bath. Her eyes searched eagerly for someone. Slowly a horse and rider emerged from that shady spot and came toward her. Both riders reined in at the same moment. "A bit warm for such vigorous exercise, is it not?" Radbourne observed mildly.

"Oh, Giles, I was so afraid you would be gone already!" Althea blurted out with incurable honesty.

The viscount smiled reassuringly at Thea and laid a large hand over hers. "Scarcely likely, I assure you." He paused and his eyes searched hers intently. "Has something happened to overset you since I last saw you?" he demanded.

It seemed so natural to confide in him, that Anthea did not hesitate. "Lord Sterne, of course. You will have heard that he is in Bath. Apparently my brother has given Sterne permission to *attempt* to pay his addresses to Cal," Anthea told him bitterly.

"Attempt?" Giles raised an eyebrow. "Have you or have you not sent the fellow about his business, and what does he say to that?"

She hesitated, and Radbourne insisted that they ride over to the trees, dismount and tether the horses, and make themselves comfortable before she tried to explain. "Now, then," he said at last, when they were seated against a tree with his arm around her shoulder and her head against his chest. "Tell me all about it."

"He refuses to leave Bath," Anthea began abruptly. "And I told him that he should be denied entrance to the house, but Sterne only laughed and said he would contrive to encounter Calandra elsewhere. The poor girl is terrified of him, and I shan't say I blame her. There is something about the fellow that makes me want to hide behind locked doors and never see him again in my life. I should think there are very few things he would stick at doing. What angers me most is that my brother should have been such a nodcock as to encourage Sterne! That makes my position particularly difficult, you know. What *shall* I do?" she asked, turning to look up at his face.

"This," Giles said, and proceeded to kiss her.

"Do be serious!" Anthea retorted, reluctantly drawing back.

"I am," Radbourne protested. "Marry me, and I shall undertake to protect both of you from Sterne."

"That seems a rather drastic solution," Anthea observed dryly.

As an answer, Radbourne kissed her again. His eyes held a distinct twinkle as, a moment later, he said, "I might, of course, have other things in mind, as well." He paused and, suddenly serious, asked, "Well, dear one, *will* you marry me?"

Anthea looked up at Giles, her eyes searching his for some sign that he was jesting. There was none. Her own began to fill with tears as she said in a voice scarcely above a whisper, "I can't, Giles."

His arms tightened around her. "Why not?" he asked, his voice rough with emotion. "My reputation?"

Anthea shook her head. "That would never weigh with me," she answered truthfully.

"Then what is it?" Giles demanded.

Helpless to stop herself, Anthea began to cry. She tried to make a gesture of apology and found herself caught up tight against Radbourne's chest. Gently he rocked her, and his free hand removed her bonnet, then stroked her hair as he murmured soothing sounds. All only causing Anthea to cry harder.

It was some time before she could manage to stop, and when she did, Radbourne immediately sensed the change. He stopped rocking her and pulled out his own handkerchief for Anthea to use. When he saw, however, how much her hands still shook, he refused to let Anthea have the square of cloth and lace. Instead he very gently and very efficiently dried her face and turned-up nose.

At this, Anthea managed a rather watery chuckle which, in turn, caused Giles to nod approvingly. He waited a bit, then said quietly, "Will you tell me about it?"

Anthea looked down at her hands, which once more began to shake, and said, "My father was used to beat me when I was a child. He said that I belonged to him and that he had a right to treat me however he chose. I think that he would have liked to treat my mother so, but he was afraid of her and beat me instead." Anthea raised her eyes to meet Radbourne's squarely. "I was used to think there was something terribly wrong with me, because he never beat my brother. And Nurse used to speak to Papa and ask him what had occurred, and he would tell her I had been . . . been bad, and then she would scold me as well. And I believed her. And him. He was my father and I loved him very much and if he said I had been bad, it must have been so. I was only a child! It was only years later, after my father died, that I was able to look back and see that his anger had nothing to do with me." Anthea hesitated, then forced herself to go on. "There were other things as well. Things I can scarcely remember, or want to remember. And through all of this, my Mama was used to say that I must have provoked whatever occurred." Again Anthea paused. "I almost never saw my father, except at such times. Do you wonder that I grew up afraid of him? And afraid of ever placing myself in any man's hands again?"

Steadily Anthea met Radbourne's eyes, challenging him to answer her. And as she stared, her eyes also took in his handsome face and windswept hair. His broad shoulders and powerful legs were evident under the riding coat and breeches he wore. Impossible to believe that Giles would ever hurt her, and yet equally impossible, after all these years, to simply trust. Radbourne's face seemed set in angry lines, and as the silence stretched on, Anthea began to wonder if she had lost him by her honesty. "Giles?" she said at last, a slight tremor in her voice.

In the next instant, Anthea Marwood found herself pulled roughly against Lord Radbourne's chest. His chin touched the top of her head as he replied, "Dear God! No wonder you're afraid! But I swear you need never be afraid of me." He paused and looked down at her. With measured words he went on, "Nor afraid for any children we might ever have."

She looked up at him. "But I can't help being afraid," Anthea said seriously. "Don't you see? I find myself wavering between believing I'm the only one in the world that this has ever happened to, and believing that *all* families inevitably come to this! Did yours? Were you so unhappy also? Or was yours one of those happy, loving homes I dream about? That I find almost impossible to believe in."

He met her eyes squarely. "The truth, I imagine, is somewhere in between," he said. "I'm not sure there is such a thing as perfect happiness, and certainly not for any child. But neither can I say that I was ever misused. My father was a gentle yet strong man, completely indefatigable! He took his seat in the House of Lords far more seriously than I do, but never neglected his estates either. And my mother . . . You would have liked my mother. She wasn't very pretty and my father towered over her, but make no mistake, she ran the household. She adored my father and he adored her and she always had time for Edmond or James or myself. No visitor was so important that we couldn't see her if we needed to. And she, as much as my father, saw to the needs of our tenants."

"Edmond and James?" Anthea asked quietly.

"My brothers," he explained. "Edmond is the youngest of us and in the military now. My father bought him his colours the day he turned eighteen, for Edmond was always army-mad. Now he's a major and used to being in the thick of it. James . . . well, James is the middle brother and father himself to quite a brood. Six, at last count, I think. He's a country fellow and happy as a grig attending to his estate."

"It all sounds so wonderful," Anthea murmured.

"Does it?" Giles laughed, and there was a bitter edge to his voice. "I never realised how wonderful it was until after my father died and I discovered how much I missed him. Do you know, I can still hear his voice telling me that when I was viscount it would be my responsibility to see that my tenants were properly housed and such and that my land was wisely managed."

"And have you done that?" Thea could not help asking.

Radbourne shrugged self-consciously. "Not as well as I ought to, I suppose. At first, when my father died, I tried to see to things as well as he had. But Clarissa was forever complaining that I either deserted her in London or dragged her to dreary places she never wanted to be. Then she died, and for a time, nothing seemed to matter very much. I came out of that particular brown study at last, only to discover that my estates were being managed very well without me." Giles paused, then added, "By my mother. When I was so wild, after Clarissa died, she was the one who took the reins in hand. And I let her keep them until the day she called me in, five years ago, to tell me that she was dying."

"I wish I could have met your mother," Thea told him quietly. "She sounds like a wonderful woman."

"She was." Giles paused and chuckled. "And my mother would have liked you as well. I can just imagine her advising you to keep me under the cat's paw and embarrassing you by asking if you came of good breeding stock! But no one would have been kinder or yielded up the keys of the estates more readily." Something of Thea's unease communicated itself to Giles, and he asked, "What is it, dear one?"

"You talk of marriage so easily, and I am so afraid of it," Anthea replied frankly.

"Of me?" Giles asked.

"No. Of marriage," Anthea said honestly. "I'm frightened of finding myself in anyone's power, ever again. Besides," she added a trifle breathlessly, "there would be all sorts of complications."

"Tell me about them, dear one," Giles invited treacherously.

Anthea could not bring herself to meet his eyes. "Calandra . . . Castor," she retorted impatiently. "Although I am forever coming to cuffs with him, Castor is my brother and he would never forgive me if I married you. Nor do I doubt that his wife, Eugenia, would wash her hands of me!"

"Serious difficulties indeed!" Radbourne said lightly.

"Don't make game of me!" Thea said angrily. "These things may seem of scant consequence to you, but to me they matter very much. Can't you understand that I must have time to become accustomed to the notion of joining my life to yours? That it isn't such a simple thing?"

In answer, Giles said evenly, "Can you at least give me hope that my suit is not futile?"

To both their astonishment, Anthea replied by reaching up and drawing Radbourne's head down to hers. Then, very thoroughly, Thea kissed Giles. With a shaky laugh, Giles finally drew back and said, "Dear one, if you knew what you were about, you would never tempt me so foolishly. Or are you simply trying to alter the course of our discussion?"

Anthea's eyes began to dance as she replied, "What? A complaint? I have never been so deceived in anyone! I made sure you would like my kiss."

Involuntarily Radbourne's arms tightened their hold on her. "And so I do," he said.

A frown still creased his brow, however, and Thea reached up to stroke it away. "Don't," she said.

"Don't what?"

"Don't prose at me, or preach propriety. That *was* my answer to you." Anthea paused, and when she spoke again it was with constraint and seriousness. "You want to warn me, don't you, that I may provoke you into something we both shall regret. But I shan't. Regret it, I mean. I'm afraid of marriage and of placing myself in anyone's hands so irrevocably. And I shall need time to feel otherwise. But I am not a child. I cut my eyeteeth years ago and know very well what I am about. Can't you understand, Giles? I have lived all my life in fear. Fear of men, fear of love, fear of reaching out to anyone. Well, I'm tired of being afraid, tired of being lonely! Whatever the future brings—marriage or parting—I shan't regret anything about today! Hold me, Giles. Help me to lay my fears to rest. All of them, even the ones I can't begin to name."

"That's a great deal to ask," Radbourne said, his voice troubled. "I begin to feel as though I am just someone here to help you, as though *who* I am doesn't really matter."

Anthea snorted impatiently. "What a hen-witted notion if I ever heard one!" Then, her eyes meeting Radbourne's, her face softened and she went on more gently, "Already you're as dear to me as anyone I have ever known. A week ago I would not have believed that I could ever say such things to you as I have today. Or believed that anyone could make me want to share so much with him."

Anthea reached out one hand to stroke the viscount's cheek. Giles caught that hand and kissed it. When he saw that she made no move to withdraw, Giles bent his head and kissed her gently on the mouth. Anthea met him eagerly, her fingers gripping the shoulders of his coat, and Radbourne's arms tightened their hold on her. Slowly his fingers strayed higher, until one hand gently stroked her neck. Anthea's hands moved with a will of their own, and she found herself stroking the broad chest she was almost crushed against. Instinctively Giles gave her more room and his hand reached for the ripeness of her breasts straining against the bodice that confined them. Anthea's breath came in shorter gasps now, and it was Giles who reluctantly broke free. This time, Thea did not chide him for it. Instead she looked at him, confusion evident in her eyes. "I . . . I always thought," she said hesitantly, "that I was some sort of ice maiden, unable to be moved by any man's touch."

"And have you been touched so very often?" Giles asked gravely.

Anthea shook her head, and it was a moment before she could answer. "No, never. Save in the most casual of ways: my hand kissed, a peck on the cheek, an arm slipped round my waist in the waltz. But, Giles, neither did I ever ask or think of more! It seemed a senseless pursuit, one to be wary of."

"Because otherwise you might find your castle tower too hard to hide in anymore?" Giles suggested. Slowly Anthea nodded, and he smiled reassuringly at her. "Then I must be encouraged that you dare leave that tower for me." She started to speak, and Giles held a finger over her lips. "Don't," he said quietly. "Don't be afraid of me. I shan't press you for anything more, but you yourself said it was an answer to how you felt about me."

Anthea looked away, the old panic once more reasserting itself. Unable to bear it any longer, she got to her feet, murmuring, "I must be going now, Giles."

With little haste or apparent concern, Lord Radbourne also rose to his feet. Calmly he asked, "When shall I see you again?"

In spite of her fear, Anthea scarcely hesitated. As she named a day and time, Thea discovered that she felt not the least pang of guilt over what Castor and Eugenia would surely depreciate as impropriety—if not outright depravity. And so a small smile played about her pale face. Once more Giles kissed her hand, then lifted her easily onto her horse. As he untethered the restless mare, Anthea asked, puzzled, "Aren't you coming?"

Giles shook his head and said, a trifle wryly, "Later. I need time alone to think, dear one. Now, go, or they shall be wondering where you are."

Anthea hesitated only a moment before she nodded, then turned her horse and headed for Bath. Radbourne stood for a long time looking after her.

13

The days began to fall into a pattern. Cal was frequently in Melanie's company, either with Mrs. Balder or with Anthea. And although Bath was a quiet place with a preponderance of older people, Cal nevertheless attracted any number of admirers besides Pitney. Melanie, with her fair curls and fine features, would have had just as many save that she had a distracted air about her. An air that both Letty and Thea suspected would disappear the moment Weylin Seabrook returned to Bath.

Lord Sterne, of course, kept his promise. He was forever encountering Cal and her aunt—in the Pump Room, the theatre, at concerts, or in the park. Anthea was unfailingly aloof but polite. Calandra tried her best to emulate her aunt, but it was undeniable that some of her fear showed through. Which only whetted Sterne's appetite for more.

And Giles. Giles remained in Bath also, but save on his rides with Anthea, he rarely encoun-

tered her or her niece. Instead, he appeared to
devote his attention to Mrs. Margaret Taggert,
who also lingered in Bath. It was a situation
which was satisfactory to neither lady and something of a puzzle to both. But it was, for Giles,
an unaccustomed attempt to throw dust in the
eyes of the local tattle-boxes and in that way
protect Anthea from the danger of any of them
suspecting her liaison with him.

Eugenia and Castor, meanwhile, sent frequent
letters admonishing Calandra to "come to her
senses" and Anthea not to "put nonsense in the
girl's head." But so long as Thea continued to
frank her niece, the Marwoods seemed content
to leave her in Anthea's care. Weylin was a more
congenial, if rather erratic correspondent. Anthea
began to find herself looking forward to his letters almost as much as Calandra did, for they
were a pleasant, uncomplicated respite from her
own problems.

For Anthea Marwood was no closer than she
had ever been to a solution about Giles. Their
rides had become somewhat . . . cooler, less passion and more intimate conversation. Giles
seemed determined that Anthea should come to
know and trust him before he would risk passion taking them to a point that Thea might
later regret. But there were times when Anthea
felt, with despair, that it was hopeless. To trust
meant to be vulnerable, and she was not in the
least certain that she wanted to be vulnerable
again. And yet the thought of losing Giles was
more than Thea could bear. So she went on
meeting him, went on trying to learn how to
trust, and in the process became, in the eyes of

her friends, far more accessible. Anthea had always been accounted an amiable girl, never
above her company, but with a reserve that
only added to her consequence. As the summer
wore on, however, Letty Balder in particular
noted the increased warmth in Thea's manner
and drew her own pleased conclusions. Agatha
Lawley, on the other hand, perceived only that
her dearest Anthea was inclined to turn less and
less to her companion for conversation or anything else. And Agatha Lawley began to worry a
great deal about the future. Calandra only noted
that her dearest aunt appeared a trifle distracted
of late and resolved to be as little trouble as
possible to her.

So little trouble was Cal, in fact, that Anthea
was quite surprised one morning to have the
child burst into her room without warning. "Aunt
Thea!" Calandra said breathlessly. "I've just received the most marvellous letter!"

"*Not* from your father, I collect," Anthea observed dryly.

"No, from Wey. He says his father is much
recovered and he expects to rejoin us any day
now. I think," Cal added, a roguish twinkle in
her eyes, "that he can't bear to be parted from
Melanie for so long. Not that he says so, of
course. But I have known him all my life, and
there is something about the way he asks me to
give his regards to her that makes me suspect
more than mere politeness."

Anthea laughed. "I shouldn't be in the least
surprised to discover that you were right," she
said. "Or that Melanie returned that regard!
Shall we go find Letty and her daughter and

inform them of the good news? At this hour I don't doubt we may discover them at the Pump Room.''

In answer, Cal hugged her aunt and hurried to her own room to change. A short time later, the two ladies were happily recounting Weylin's letter to the Balders. Melanie was all happiness and Letty quiet approval. Well aware of the needs of youth, Letty and Thea soon left the girls alone to chatter and speculate. Letty herself had a new admirer, and within minutes Anthea found herself alone on the far side of the room, a circumstance which did not trouble her in the least. She was completely unaware, however, of the lovely picture she made standing there with her flaming hair and fashionably cut walking dress of a striking shade of green. ''My dear Miss Marwood, how delightful to see you today,'' a voice said from behind her.

Stiffening, Anthea turned and tilted her chin up slightly. ''Good day, Lord Sterne,'' she said in a voice that seemed a trifle bored.

Sterne swallowed his anger as he bowed. ''Your niece appears to be in excellent spirits,'' he observed.

''She is,'' Anthea confirmed coolly. ''She had a letter that conveyed very good news to her.''

''What a coincidence!'' Lord Sterne said, all amazement. ''I, too, have had such a letter!''

''Indeed?'' Once more Thea's tone conveyed exquisite boredom.

Sterne's eyes danced appreciatively as he replied. ''Yes. In fact, I quite believe I shall share it with you. After all, it was written by your brother. Or, more likely perhaps, his wife.''

Anthea was shaken, but none of this showed on her face as she nodded politely. "My dear lady," Sterne said in evident admiration, "what *savoir-faire*! When I know you must be wishing me at Jericho. If you were ten or more years younger ... But you are not!" He paused. "I must not, however, forget the news, since I am persuaded that you will find your brother's—or his wife's—advice a fascinating as I do. He urges me, you see, to bring Miss Calandra to the point, at once, and to tolerate no more of this missish nonsense. It is, I think, rather in the nature of a command. A command I think I should heed, don't you agree, Miss Marwood?"

It was several moments before Anthea could contain her temper sufficiently to answer. When she did so, however, she sounded as calm as ever. "By all means, put your fortune to the test, my lord! I have no objection if you choose to make a formal offer to my niece. I warn you, however, that so long as Calandra is in my care, you must abide by her answer. Do you understand me, my lord?"

Sterne inclined his head. "My dear lady, I am quite certain we understand each other perfectly! How could it be otherwise when we have been at such pains to express our thoughts so clearly? As for your suggestion, why, I shall call in the morning to ... put my fortune, as you call it, to the test. I trust your servants *will* have orders to admit me?"

Anthea nodded, a slight pallor the only indication of her inward unease. "Of course," she said coolly.

Sterne bowed, his smile very broad as he said, "Until then, dear lady, *adieu.*"

Her first thoughts, when Sterne was gone, were of Giles. She must send word to him that she could not come for their ride together. Anthea's second thoughts were of a grim determination that after Cal had refused Sterne's offer, she would help speed him on his way with a few choice words of her own! Anthea's third thoughts were of Giles. If only it were not so difficult to see him!

"Wool-gathering?" a voice laughed nearby. Anthea opened her eyes to discover Letty regarding her with a little amusement. "I hope," Mrs. Balder went on, "that your thoughts were pleasant ones?"

Decisively Anthea shook her head. "Scarcely! Lord Sterne intends to make Cal a formal offer tomorrow morning."

"You don't fear she'll accept him, do you?" Letty asked with some surprise. "I thought her quite agreed with you that Sterne was far too old and far too unsavoury a fellow."

"She does agree with me," Anthea confirmed. "My concern is rather what his lordship may do after Cal turns him down."

Letty spread her shapely hands in protest. "Well, what *can* he do? Abduct her? Sterne must know you would never stand for that!"

In spite of herself, Anthea laughed. "You're right, Letty. I'm being absurd. I just wish Castor had never given his blessing to this horrid suit."

"Well, never mind," Letty said soothingly. "After Calandra refuses Sterne tomorrow, you may quite safely vent your spleen on the fellow, and I warrant you'll feel much better for it."

"How unhandsome of me *that* would be!" Anthea retorted, choking back a gurgle of laughter.

"But how much fun!" Letty riposted. "And why not? You can scarcely wish to remain on terms with the fellow."

Miss Marwood answered slowly, "No, but neither am I certain that I wish to have Sterne for an enemy. There are times when I am quite afraid of him." Abruptly Anthea shook herself. "Enough of this or I shall fall into a brown study! Come, let us fetch the girls. Cal and I have an appointment with my *modiste*. I am determined the child shall have a complete wardrobe for the first time in her life! Can you imagine, Letty, never wearing anything but hand-me-overs and sharing one's few things with one's sisters?"

Letty Balder shuddered. She was all sympathy. "I don't understand, however," she said, a small frown appearing between her eyebrows, "*why*. I never thought your brother wealthy, but I should scarcely have called him a pauper, either."

"My brother and his wife," Anthea replied dryly, "are quite comfortably circumstanced, I assure you. But, as they have frequently informed me, they do not consider that a reason for improvidence. Particularly with five daughters to provide for. After all, why waste one's blunt on expensive dresses that children cannot possibly appreciate? It would only spoil them. Of course, as each girl comes of age and is brought out, she does acquire a wardrobe suitable for her Season. Castor and Eugenia are no fools.

They can well imagine what the *ton* would say if they did otherwise. And it is scarcely a waste, since the dresses can afterwards be sent home to be worn by the younger girls there. Once they have outlived their usefulness in London."

"Well, they may call it prudence," Letty said with a distinct sniff, "but I think it quite shabby, all the same. I'm thankful that Mr. Balder, before he died, never took such an absurd notion into his head!"

Anthea gurgled with laughter. "As if you would have tolerated it, Letty!"

Mrs. Balder laughed also but said, "I shan't keep you any longer if you've an appointment with Fanny. She has a dreadful way of scolding if one is the least bit late—and one always is. For a *modiste* she is terribly unservile!"

"And I am convinced that that is no small part of her success!" Anthea retorted amiably.

A few minutes later the two friends parted as Anthea swept Calandra off to a delightful session of looking at fabrics and patterns and ordering dresses. It would have been difficult to say which of the ladies enjoyed herself more.

Eventually Anthea was able to sit down to compose a note to Giles. It took several efforts, and even the final result did not entirely please her. For it was unthinkable that Anthea should discuss Calandra's affairs in such a missive. Well, it would have to do. A simple cancellation of their ride. As soon as it was sealed, a footman was dispatched to carry the message to Lord Radbourne's hotel.

At York House, Peter, the young footman, was informed that the Viscount Radbourne was out and his valet had been given the evening off. It was to be inferred, therefore, that his lordship expected to be out quite late. One was advised to leave the, er, missive in the care of the staff and rest assured that his lordship would receive it directly he returned to York House.

Peter hesitated, and the fellow shrugged eloquently. "Of course, if you *prefer* to wait and deliver the message personally, you may do so. *Over there.*"

These last words were accompanied by a gesture toward a chair that stood in a shadowed corner of the foyer. Peter looked at it, then at the *concierge*, and swallowed. Another shrug and—being so young, you understand—Peter was thoroughly routed. He stammered something to the effect that *of course* he would leave the message in the care of the fellow and thank you very much indeed! And with that Peter beat a hasty retreat to Laura Place and the pretty little upstairs maid who had been casting up her eyes at him of late.

He need not have worried. When Lord Radbourne returned to York House, far earlier than expected, and in company with a lady, the *concierge* instantly presented him with the message. "For you, my lord," he said obsequiously.

"Who is it from?" Maggie demanded suspiciously. "Open it, Giles!" she commanded when he shrugged.

Giles merely looked at her. He turned the missive over in his hand, then said curtly, "Wait here for me, Maggie. I shan't be above ten minutes."

Maggie Taggert forced herself to smile and say, "Of course."

"Good."

While the viscount casually disappeared up the stairs, the *concierge* subjected Mrs. Taggert to a swift but careful covert scrutiny. *Not* a person worthy of, or requiring, his personal attention. In spite of her presence with Lord Radbourne. And as the fellow was rather jealous of his consequence, having but recently been promoted, he summoned an underling and retreated to a far corner of the room, where he seemed very busy. Maggie, whose sharp eyes missed none of this, was not pleased. By the time Giles reappeared, her temper was in shreds. Nor was it improved when Giles summoned the *concierge* and said, "Please have this reply delivered to Miss Anthea Marwood, Laura Place."

14

The drawing room at Miss Marwood's house in Laura Place was furnished as much with comfort as with elegance in mind. And yet, neither of the two ladies in it appeared at ease that morning. It should have been three ladies, of course, but Anthea had banished Miss Lawley at the first sign that Agatha intended to be difficult. Not that Miss Lawley would *dream* of so far putting herself forward as to advise dear Miss Marwood's niece as to what to do about her suitor, but Agatha did think it such a pity Anthea's brother was not here to provide wiser counsel than she could give. For it was quite evident that the child, Calandra, stood in need of her father's guiding hand. Not that one meant to say that Miss Anthea was deficient in understanding, for such a charge would be patently absurd! But men, after all, could not suffer from missish notions or absurd flights of fancy.

At this point with great effort, Anthea managed to simply request Miss Lawley to *go out* and do the shopping! Always eager to be of service, Miss Lawley was only too happy to oblige.

"However can you bear that woman?" Calandra demanded as soon as Agatha was gone.

Thea answered with very little hesitation, "She has been with me ... oh, forever it seems! Do you know why I chose her? When my mother was ill, Agatha was used to come and visit and sit with her—and listen with endless patience to Mama's complaints. I do not know what I should have done without those visits. And after Mama's death, I knew I must have *someone* to lend me countenance. Though I must admit that it does seem absurd that now, at my age, I am not allowed to live alone! And yet I would not simply turn out Agatha, even if I could. I have too much reason to remember her kindliness."

"I see that," Cal agreed frankly, "but however do you bear her conversation? Her absurd notions? Her *utter* propriety!"

Anthea laughed and shook her head. "I simply don't regard it when she proses at me. Why should I? It is not as though she can do anything except prose. Nor need you regard her. When Lord Sterne arrives, you need only listen as he makes you his offer, then accept or decline it."

"Accept him?" Cal demanded indignantly. "That fat flawn?"

"Hush! I hear him coming!" Anthea warned her niece as footsteps approached.

For perhaps the twentieth time, Anthea smoothed her skirt and then folded her hands in her lap. She was determined that his lordship should not put her out of countenance. Calandra could not so easily command her emotions, and as Jeffries announced Lord Sterne, Cal turned quite pale. Indeed her hand trembled as the fellow made his bow. "Charming, my dear, you look absolutely charming," he told her. To Thea he added, "I presume you've told her why I'm here?" At Thea's nod, he went on, "Then, my dear Calandra, you shan't be surprised by my next request. Miss Calandra Marwood, will you do me the honour of becoming my wife?"

Calandra curtseyed, then met his eyes steadily as she replied, "No, my lord, I will not. Nor do I understand why you persist in what you must know to be a futile enterprise."

Sterne's smile did not reach his eyes. "Your father favours my suit. I have no doubt he could find the means to compel you if he chose."

Calandra darted a frightened look at Thea, who said, "No, Lord Sterne, he could not. *I* have the means, you see, to compel Castor to leave his daughter in my care. And so long as she is in my care, no one will compel her to wed against her will. I'm sorry if you gambled on my brother's goodwill. If so, you have lost."

Sterne viewed Anthea from head to toe, then addressed Calandra, his tone contemptuous. "Do you intend to become an ape-leader, then? Like your aunt? All shrivelled-up bitterness at men?"

"I scarcely think that likely," Anthea answered calmly. "I fear Calandra will find herself more than enough suitors and no doubt will settle down happily to married life before she is far past her coming of age. It seems more likely to me, my lord, that it is you who will end up alone."

Sterne regarded the elder Miss Marwood coolly. "Quite the fishwife, aren't you?" he said. "But I ask myself why? What have I done to incur such enmity?"

Thea met his eyes frankly. "I dislike men who find joy in frightening young girls."

"Hearsay! Nonsense! Gossip, my dear!" Lord Sterne dismissed the charge with a snap of his fingers. "I've no doubt my reputation has been painted quite black for you, but I beg you will not rely on mere gossip. Judge me, instead, for yourself. Have I not been all attention to Miss Calandra? Have I not sent her the most tempting of gifts? Are these the acts of an ogre? So let us hear no more of these absurd tales you have been told!"

With difficulty, Anthea kept her temper in check. "I do not refer to gossip, my lord. I speak from my own knowledge. I am sure you do not recall a certain evening, twelve years ago, but I do. You were *on the go* but scarcely *castaway* and you had your fun frightening *me*. Can you wonder, then, that I do not welcome your attentions toward my niece?"

Shaken, but only slightly, Sterne retorted, "Did I? You must have encouraged me, then. Is that what this is all about? Pique because I turned my back on you twelve years ago, Miss Marwood? Such jealousy! Surely it is unworthy of you." He clucked over it. "And you would sacrifice your niece's happiness for such a reason?"

"Why, you . . . you . . ." Words failed Calandra. "How dare you stand there spouting such nonsense? I wish you will go away and never see us again!"

Sterne looked at her calmly. "If you detest me so thoroughly, my dear, why are you wearing my brooch?"

"Brooch?"

"Yes. With little amethysts and sapphires. I made sure you would like it, and it seems you do."

Calandra looked with horror at the piece of jewelry on her chest. "I thought Pitney sent it! Or Roger." Her voice was scarcely above a whisper.

Sterne smiled perfunctorily. "Nevertheless, it was I who did so. And you are wearing it now. Surely that gives me hope?"

With a vehement gesture, Cal reached for the brooch to unpin it. "If it is yours," she said, "then you shall have it back. This instant!"

"Don't bother," Sterne said calmly. "For I shan't take it back, you know. I wish to think of it being in your possession."

"If you don't take it, I shall throw it away," she warned him.

"Fine," Lord Sterne said, spreading his hands in an amiable gesture. "I daresay your servants will have a great deal to gossip over if you do, but that is certainly your affair. Do as you wish. But don't try to return the brooch to me, for I shan't accept it."

At this point, Thea judged it time to intervene. "Please leave, my lord," she said coolly. "You have made your offer to Calandra and she has refused it. There can be nothing more for you to say to either of us. It is, perhaps, unnecessary for me to add that you will not be welcome again in this house. Jeffries will show you out."

Sterne bowed. As he left, he was outwardly calm, but anyone well acquainted with his lordship would have recognised the signs of his rage. Anyone *intimately* acquainted with Sterne would have begun to anticipate his revenge.

15

The young man entering the White Hart and requesting a room might have been any provincial buck visiting Bath. He was, in fact, Weylin Seabrook, and he carried himself with a far greater degree of self-assurance than had been evident a month before. The clerk at the desk expressed a gratified pleasure at once more having the opportunity to serve young Seabrook. A certain chambermaid, moreover, giggled in a most unbecoming way at the direction to prepare a room for the gentleman. Meanwhile, young Seabrook was invited to enjoy a neat little luncheon in one of the public rooms. Weylin graciously agreed.

Weylin was, in point of fact, greatly enjoying himself. His boots might be dusty from his journey, but his riding coat was remarkably well cut for having come from a country tailor, and no fault could have been found with the fit of his breeches. Nor was it his appearance alone that buoyed Seabrook's spirits. His visit home, which had begun in fear for his father's health, had gone remarkably well. For one thing, the elder Seabrook's hold on life had been far more tenacious than anyone expected. And that hold had rapidly become even stronger upon the discovery by Weylin's parents that he was not about to offer for Calandra Marwood. The Marwoods and the Seabrooks were not, you see, on speaking terms. This was, Weylin could not help feeling, a pity, but it was a fact past mending. He was shrewd enough to guess, however, that once Cal and all her sisters were safely married— to someone other than Weylin—then both Mr. Marwood and Arthur Seabrook would somehow contrive to patch up their quarrel. Neither parent had succeeded in banning the friendship between Cal and Wey, but only because the pair had been discreet in their meetings. Discreet, that is, until Weylin had suddenly taken it into his head to accompany Calandra and her aunt to Bath.

It was therefore with great relief that the Seabrooks received Weylin's assurances that Calandra Marwood remained merely a friend. This assurance was followed, however, by the information that Weylin had formed an attachment to some chit by the name of Melanie Balder. Had Mrs. Seabrook been of a disposition to have spasms, she would no doubt have succumbed. Nor would it have been surprising had Mr. Seabrook suffered a relapse. Instead, however, Weylin was simply directed to tell them more about the girl and her family. Encouraged by this mild response, Weylin happily did so. It was not, the elder Seabrooks later agreed, a connection they could entirely like. Nevertheless, it was certainly preferable to having the Marwoods for in-laws. Both had, moreover, a high degree of respect for Anthea Marwood's good sense, and if *she* liked the family, that must count heavily in the girl's favour.

And so, by the end of Weylin's visit home, the elder Seabrooks had resigned themselves to the attachment and even formed plans for a visit to Bath later in the year. It is scarcely surprising, therefore, that Weylin was in excellent spirits as he sat down to his luncheon at the White Hart. As soon as he had a chance to change out of his riding clothes, he must call on Cal and Melanie. His parents had asked, and Weylin was sensible enough to agree, that he wait before speaking to Melanie's guardian. It was only fair to give themselves both time to be certain of their own minds. Nevertheless, it could not be denied that the question of which of his changes of apparel would most impress Melanie greatly occupied Weylin's mind. He had but recently learned to tie his cravat in the *Mathematical*, a style which must, he felt, proclaim that he was not altogether a contemptible fellow. So preoccupied was Weylin that he did not immediately notice the voices which intruded from the next room. It was only when he heard a familiar name that his attention was caught.

". . . Marwood chit! Damme, but I'll not stand for it!"

"Indeed, Perry?" a feminine voice purred. "And what shall you do about it? Kidnap the girl?

Carry her off and ravish her? Doing it much too brown, my dear. Even her complacent father will scarcely forgive you for that."

There was a pause before the silky, masculine voice replied, "Nevertheless, Miss Calandra Marwood must be taught a lesson. I should like your help, Maggie."

"What do you intend to do?" the woman asked warily.

"A simple deceit," the man protested airily. "A slight scare should suffice. Let her think she is coming to meet you somewhere, and I shall be there instead."

A pause. "Why should she come to meet me? And what will you really do, once she is there?"

"Scruples, Maggie, my dear? How astonishing!" The voice was steel cloaked in velvet. "Will it ease your conscience if I tell you that I have nothing dishonourable in mind? Perhaps I shall merely read her a scold, then send her home again."

"And how does that serve you, Perry?" Maggie asked suspiciously.

"I wish to leave her feeling as foolish as I did today. As for why she will meet you, there is the matter of Giles Radbourne, you know," the man replied easily.

"Giles?" The woman's voice was crisply alert now. "What do you mean?"

Weylin could easily imagine the fellow coolly studying his fingernails as he replied, "Even Miss Calandra must be aware that you are, shall we say, the viscount's *dear* companion. Presumably she is also aware, as you are, of her aunt's secret assignations with Radbourne."

"How do you know about that?" Maggie whispered.

The voice that answered sent a chill down Weylin's spine. "Did you think I wouldn't know? How naive of you! It would also be naive of you to assume I didn't know about Lord Farold and *your*, er, *meetings* with him. I am persuaded Radbourne would find that information *most* interesting."

"What is it you wish me to do?" Maggie asked listlessly.

"Merely write Miss Calandra a note telling her that you have something important to impart to her regarding her aunt and Viscount Radbourne. Ask her to meet you at, let me see . . . at the Blue Goose. A small inn at the edge of Bath," he explained kindly. A pause; then, "Come, come, Maggie, my dear! Where is your sense of humor?"

"Sometimes I think I hate you, Sterne," she answered quietly.

He laughed. "What? Have I ceased to be 'Perry' to you? Never mind. Just don't forget what I promised to do to you if you fail me. I should enjoy having you as my captive and ravishing you day and night! Now, go and write that note."

A door slammed and the man laughed again. Weylin considered and dismissed the notion of breaking in upon the fellow. Instead he resolved to hit upon some way to outwit the pair.

A short time later, Weylin Seabrook presented

himself at the house on Laura Place. Anthea and Calandra were out, and he was directed to look for them at Mrs. Balder's address, a circumstance which could not be said to distress Weylin. Particularly as he was so fortunate as to find Cal and Melanie quite alone when he arrived there. And they were gratifyingly pleased to see him and impressed with his coat of blue superfine and primrose pantaloons.

"You look all the crack yourself," Weylin told Cal.

She laughed. "It scarcely seems real sometimes! And how long it shall last, I don't know. Mama will be furious when she learns I've whistled Sterne and his marriage settlement down the wind. I only hope she may not make me go home at once."

"Surely she won't!" Melanie protested. "No one could expect you to marry Lord Sterne."

Cal smiled and shook her head, but Weylin was more blunt. "It's plain you ain't met Cal's mother, then," he snorted. "But what exactly *has* happened, Cal?"

She shrugged and turned away to look out the window. "He made me an offer, I rejected it, and Aunt Thea has forbidden him the house."

So that's what he meant, Weylin said to himself. Aloud he asked, "I say, you haven't received any notes ... *odd* notes ... from anyone today, have you?"

Melanie and Calandra exchanged a look; then Cal let out her breath. "How did you know? This came just before I left Aunt Thea's house. Only Melanie and I know of it."

Weylin took the note held out to him and read it quickly. It confirmed his suspicions.

My dear Miss Calandra Marwood,
    If you wish to protect your aunt's reputation, meet me at the Blue Goose at nine o'clock this evening. Anyone may tell you how to find it. I advise you to be there.
                    Mrs. Margaret Taggert

"What shall I do?" Cal asked Weylin when he had finished reading the note.

"Nothing. I shall go in your place," he replied.

"*What?*"

"It's a plot," Weylin explained patiently. "I overheard Sterne and this woman, Mrs. Taggert, talking at the White Hart. If *you* go, you'll find Sterne waiting, not her. He said he plans to frighten you, but I should like to surprise him, instead."

"But he'll be furious!" Calandra protested.

Weylin nodded. "What can he do to me? We shall, after all, be in a public place."

"What if he should be angry and come looking for me?" Calandra asked fearfully.

"Stay here, where he can't find you," Weylin answered promptly. "And if you're really afraid, don't tell *anyone* you're here, until I return." He paused and turned to Melanie. "Give out to the servants and your mother that Cal has left and then hide her in your room. As soon as I have sent Lord Sterne about his business and am sure it is safe, I shall come back and tell you."

Calandra was still hesitant. "Perhaps I ought to tell Aunt Thea and ask her advice."

"No." Weylin was positive. "I wish Lord Sterne to know that you have *some* man to protect you, even if your father will not."

"Just what is it you have in mind?" Cal asked cautiously.

His eyes brimming with mischief, Wey replied, "Why, I shall simply take your place, Cal. Look, we're much of the same height and build, and if I wore your clothes and a hat with a veil, no one would know I wasn't you. At least not in the dark! Just think of Sterne's face when he discovers that instead of a frightened, helpless young girl, he's got *me* to contend with!"

Cal laughed, but Melanie asked nervously, "But what if his lordship should turn nasty? And try to harm you?"

Gravely Wey answered, "How can he? I've told you we shall be in a public place. And in any case, I'm accounted a very handy fellow with my fives."

"That," Cal explained dryly, "I collect is boxing cant. All right. We'll do as you say. But do you think I should send a note to Aunt Thea telling her where I am? Or what's afoot?"

Weylin shook his head. "No," he said positively. "She would only try to stop us. In any event, I shall be back before she has time to worry. Just send her a note, perhaps, that you will be here very late. Now, would Sterne recognise the dress you have on?"

Cal nodded. "Yes, for I wore it this morning." She hesitated, then went on, "I also have a brooch in my reticule. It was a gift from him, but I didn't know it. You could wear that, and he would be certain to think it was I."

"Famous!" Weylin crowed. "Melanie, have you a hat with a veil I could wear?"

Shyly she nodded. "And clothes Calandra can borrow until you return with hers."

"Good," he replied, well satisfied. "Cal, write that note, then give me your clothes. I shall deliver the note to Miss Marwood's house, then go to a friend I know. He will let me change there and ask no questions. I don't wish to risk Mrs. Taggert seeing me at the White Hart."

A short time later, Melanie let Weylin out of the house herself. It was, he could not but feel, the start of a marvellous adventure.

At precisely nine o'clock that evening, a young woman entered the courtyard of the Blue Goose. She moved gracefully, with dainty steps, and with an air of hesitancy that was only reinforced by the heavy veil she wore. Here for an assignation, she must be, the ostler told himself knowledgeably. Aye, and her first, at that, from the looks of things. Ah, well, it wasn't *his* concern if she'd come to meet the gen'lemun standing in the shadows! No, not even if it was an elopement they planned, as he more'n half suspected.

The young woman continued making her way toward the doorway of the inn. As the light fell on her dress, a brooch gleamed and a voice floated across the courtyard, "Miss Calandra Marwood?"

The young woman paused and looked about and slowly nodded. As she did so, the figure in the shadows stepped forward with a nod to some unseen companion. And in the next moment

Weylin felt himself being seized from behind, a vile liquid being forced down his throat, and just before he lost consciousness, Weylin was aware of being thrust into a carriage and the door shut behind him!

16

Anthea Marwood was not a woman generally given to alarm. Cal's desire to enjoy a long, comfortable visit with Melanie Balder struck her as an excellent sign that Cal had recovered from Lord Sterne's visit. Thea's only concern was that Cal should not impose on the Balders. In this case, since Cal intended to return to Laura Place well after dark, Letty would be put to the trouble of having a footman accompany her. Anthea determined to spare Letty the need and set out, late in the evening, to collect Cal herself. Her calm, however, was swiftly replaced by alarm at Letty's first words. "Do come in, Anthea! But where is Calandra?"

Out of reflex, Thea looked about her friend's cozy drawing room and said, "Why, I looked to find her here, Letty. When did she leave?"

"This afternoon, or so I understand. I was out, you see. I believe she left with young Seabrook. Why? Is something amiss?"

"How odd," Thea said, half to herself. "I had

a note from Cal that said she meant to be with Melanie all day. She might, I suppose, have changed her mind and gone somewhere with Wey, but to do what? And surely Cal ought to have returned by now. Perhaps Melanie may know what their plans were. May I see her?''

Letty Balder spread her hands helplessly. "She's laid down on her bed with the headache, poor child. Indeed, I gave her a strong dose of laudanum scarcely half an hour ago, and she will be fast asleep now. She even took supper on a tray in her room, she was feeling so ill!''

Rather distractedly Anthea gave some sort of sympathetic reply and almost immediately took her leave. "I must call on Weylin and see what he can tell me of this affair,'' she told Letty bluntly.

A short time later Miss Anthea Marwood entered the White Hart. She was still more puzzled than truly alarmed. "I should like to speak with Weylin Seabrook,'' she told the clerk at the desk. "I believe him to be staying here.''

The fellow studied the lady before him. She was well-dressed and carried herself with the air of a well-bred lady. Nevertheless, it was *not* the policy of the White Hart to encourage *female persons* to call on male guests. "He is not in at the moment,'' the clerk replied curtly. "Nor has he been in for the past several hours. We cannot tell you where he has gone,'' the clerk added severely before the lady could be so impertinent as to ask.

"It is most urgent that I locate Mr. Seabrook,'' Anthea persisted. "I assure you I know the boy well.''

The clerk drew himself fully erect. Not for nothing had he long held this position of chief night clerk for the White Hart. *He* was not a paltry fellow to be deceived by an air of respectability. Ladies did not call on gentlemen at their hotels—not at this time of night they didn't! Fixing Anthea with his most quelling stare, he said loftily, "That is what they *all* say! I repeat: we cannot help you. And may I add that a female of your age ought to be ashamed—pursuing such a nice young gentleman as Mr. Seabrook!"

Outrage warred with humour, and the latter won. To the clerk's astonishment, Anthea chuckled. "Very well, I shan't trouble you any further. Your suspicions are quite mistaken, you know, but I cannot bring myself to disapprove of the way you protect your guests."

With whatever dignity she could still summon up, Anthea turned to leave. It was very late and very dark out, and, it seemed to Thea, quite unlike Cal to so worry her aunt. Her head rather bowed, Anthea did not see the gentleman until she collided with him. "Oh, I'm sorry, pray excuse me," she murmured automatically.

Instead of allowing her to pass, however, the gentleman bluntly demanded, "What are you doing here, Miss Marwood? What's amiss?"

"Giles! Lord Radbourne," Anthea hastily corrected herself, conscious of the interested stares they were drawing. Then, perceiving the viscount's companion, she added, "And Mrs. Taggert. Good evening."

But Radbourne had no patience for the amenities. "What has happened to overset you?" he repeated. "And what the devil are you doing here?"

"I came to see Weylin," Anthea replied, her brain refusing to put clearer words to her tongue.

"Indeed?" Mrs. Taggert purred with precisely the same degree of arch amusement that the night clerk's assistant had shown. "How ... *interesting.*"

"How unconventional," Giles agreed. "And quite unlike you, Miss Marwood."

Casting caution to the winds, Thea said urgently, "I must speak with you alone, Lord Radbourne!"

"Yes, of course," he said at once. "Maggie—"

"No!" she said, cutting him short. "I wish to hear this. Or would you prefer that I consider ways to broadcast Miss Marwood's indiscreet behaviour here tonight?"

Giles hesitated, but Thea did not. "What difference does it make what she says about me? I must speak with you alone!"

Curtly Giles dismissed Maggie, who angrily retreated to her room. Any misgivings she had felt earlier about aiding Perry were gone in her rage at such treatment. It was only a few minutes later, however, that Giles burst into her rooms in a rage himself. Miss Marwood was close behind.

Seizing Maggie by her shoulders, Radbourne demanded, "Where is Calandra Marwood?"

From behind him, with an air of bewilderment, Thea asked, "How can Mrs. Taggert possibly know?"

Determined to brazen it out, Maggie echoed

Anthea. "Yes, Giles. How could I possibly know anything about the girl?"

"Because you've been far too smug this evening," Giles retorted grimly. "And because I suspect Lord Sterne's hand in this and I know you to have taken part in his pranks before. Moreover, I've taken the precaution of speaking with the clerk downstairs, and he informs me you not only spoke with Sterne today, but you sent a message to be delivered directly into the hand of Miss Calandra Marwood!"

"How . . . how could he possibly know that?" Maggie gasped. "I sent my maid!"

"A maid," Giles said evenly, "who I understand is about to retire from your service to marry the night clerk here at the White Hart. She told him all about it. So, Maggie, you had better tell *me* the rest."

"I . . . I can't," Maggie whispered, wetting her lips with her tongue. "Perry would kill me."

Giles bowed. "Then I suggest you retire to the country for a while, where he cannot find you. Or to the Continent. For while I am not convinced that Sterne would kill you, I am quite certain that I shall—unless you tell me everything *at once!*"

As she looked at the rage in Radbourne's eyes, Maggie had no trouble believing him. A moment later she capitulated and began to explain. "It was to be a jest. Played upon Miss Calandra. Perry wished to humiliate the chit for scorning him. I was to write—did write—a note setting a rendez-vous, and Perry was to take my place there. I swear he told me he only meant to rake her down and send her home. I shouldn't be in the least surprised if she is there now. The appointment was for nine o'clock, and it is well past that now."

Anthea looked at Giles, her mind unable to think. His voice was rough with reassurance as he said, "We shall stop at Laura Place, and if she is not there, we shall go on to the place of rendez-vous, Anthea." He turned back to Maggie, and the menace in his voice was unmistakable as he said, *"Where was it to be, Maggie?"*

"The Blue Goose," Maggie said faintly. "Perry said it was a small inn just to the north of Bath."

Now, finally, Giles let go of Maggie's shoulders. Very deliberately he said, "I advise you to get out of Bath at once, Maggie."

As they left the White Hart, Anthea asked Giles anxiously, "Do you think Mrs. Taggert told us the truth?"

"We shall soon know," Giles said grimly. "But I believe so."

With that, Anthea had to be content. Radbourne might have added, though he did not, that he was not nearly so certain that Sterne had told Maggie the truth of his plans. It sounded far too tame a scheme for the blackguard.

At Laura Place, his fears were confirmed. Calandra had still not returned and it was now close upon midnight. They stayed only long enough for Thea to provide herself with a warm cloak, and then they were off for the Blue Goose. The night was not particularly chilly, but Anthea shivered, grateful that Giles was with her.

At the Blue Goose they were met by stony denials that anyone had seen a young lady such as Calandra arrive. Or Lord Sterne. It was only as they stood in the innyard, debating what to do next, that the ostler approached them. "Beggin' yer pardon, m'lord, m'lady, but I heard you was askin' after a young girl?"

"Yes, yes, we were," Giles said quickly. "About so tall. Blond. Dressed . . . How was she dressed, Anthea?"

"A walking dress of blue. Did you see her?" Thea asked.

"Aye." The ostler nodded reluctantly. "And I seen a brooch wi' little sparkly stones."

"That was she!" Thea said quietly. "But why was she wearing the brooch, I wonder? Never mind. Tell us—where did she go? What happened to her?"

The ostler looked away, then down at the ground. "She came to meet a gen'lemun, I think. Leastways she left the inn in 'is carriage. Travelling east, they was, ma'am." He halted, then with an air of desperation rushed on. "The gen'lemun—I think he forced 'er into 'is carriage. He rode along outside. There wasn't no time to stop 'im afore they was gone. Wi' the fastest pair of sweet goers I've ever seen!"

As Thea clutched at Radbourne's hand, he looked down at her reassuringly. "We shall catch them, I promise you. Sir, can you find us horses and a carriage?"

Before the ostler could answer, Anthea spoke. "But, Giles! Wouldn't your curricle and team of chestnuts be faster?"

Radbourne regarded her grimly for a moment before he replied. "They would be," he confirmed, "if I hadn't lent them to a friend! I had no notion, you see, of leaving Bath just yet and thought I wouldn't need them."

At this point the ostler interrupted to say rather doubtfully, "I've a curricle and pair I *could* let you hire, but, beggin' yer pardon—is it wise? I mean, be you and the lady related or somethin'? It's awful late to start a journey. Why, yer like as not to be gone overnight!"

Anthea directed a quelling look at Giles, whose eyes were brimming with laughter. "I am the girl's aunt and she is under *my* care," Thea said haughtily.

The ostler was not impressed. "Hmmph. Not very good care, was it, if you ask me," he replied.

"We didn't," Giles said curtly.

"It's not the thing!" the ostler persisted fretfully. "I oughtn't to be 'elping wi' such goings-on."

"Will it soothe your worry over the proprieties," Giles asked through gritted teeth, "if I assure you that the lady and I are betrothed *and* very shortly to be married?"

"Oh, aye, well, in that case . . ." the ostler reluctantly agreed.

"Then will you please hitch up those horses to that curricle?" Giles roared, all patience gone. "We're in a hurry!"

"Aye, aye." The fellow hastened to do as he was bid.

There was little to be said between Anthea and Giles until they were some distance down the road. As they travelled, however, Radbourne's words rankled Anthea until finally she demanded crossly, "Why did you tell that fellow such nonsense?"

"What nonsense is that, dear one?" Giles asked treacherously.

"You know very well what I mean. That ... that Banbury tale that we were about to be married," she retorted severely.

"Oh ... that." Giles shrugged. "I only said it so that he would hire out his cattle to us. You needn't regard it."

"Oh," Anthea said in a very small voice.

And why you should feel so disappointed is beyond me! she told herself crossly. You're forever telling him you're not ready to make such a decision, aren't you?

But there was no denying that her spirits *were* cast down. For the first time Anthea really began to wonder what she would do if Giles grew tired of her missishness and walked away. Dear God, never to laugh with him again! Or share with him all those thoughts that he alone never had to have explained. The thought of such a future was suddenly intolerable to Anthea. Soberly she raised her eyes to look at Radbourne, and she found him regarding her with a quizzical expression. "After this is over, I mean to have my answer," he told her quietly.

With a sigh, Thea tucked her hand into the crook of his arm. "Did you read my mind?" she asked. "Sometimes I think you must!"

Radbourne laughed harshly. "Scarcely, dear one! If I could, I would know just what to say to help you slay your fears. But I don't. I only know that, for both our sakes, matters must come to a head—and that quite soon. *Is* marriage with me such a dreadful fate to consider?"

"No." She spoke so quietly that Giles had to

turn his head to hear her. When he did, his eyes blazed with such warmth that Thea was startled. In confusion she directed him to look to the horses. "We *are* in a hurry, Giles! I'm so afraid of what Sterne may intend for Calandra. And the fellow at the inn said Sterne's horses were fast ones. By now he must be miles and miles ahead of us!"

17

In point of fact, however, Lord Sterne and his captive were not nearly so far ahead of Radbourne and Thea as the pair supposed. Unlikely as it may seem, it was no part of Sterne's plans to arrive at his destination until well after dawn. While Sterne was not oblivious of the risk of pursuit, he considered the arrival of the elder Miss Marwood, in time to see the culmination of his design, an occurrence that could only add spice to the revenge. For there was nothing Anthea Marwood would be able to do to interfere with his plans now. Not even if she arrived with Viscount Radbourne at her side. This was, Lord Sterne felt, quite the most delicious plot he had ever contrived! And he directed the coachman to set a decorous pace while he cantered alongside.

Inside the carriage, the sole occupant, Weylin, slowly regained consciousness. Fortunately for him, the dose that had been administered had been calculated to put to sleep a mere slip of a girl. Which Weylin decidedly was not. Cautiously he lifted his head and looked about him, relieved to discover that he was alone in the carriage. That meant his deception had likely not yet been discovered. A quick glance out the curtains of the carriage gave Weylin sight of a gentleman who could be no one but Lord Sterne. Even in the moonlight, it seemed to Wey that an air of degeneracy clung to the figure on horseback. Anxious not to be seen, Weylin allowed the curtain to fall back into place to cover the window of the coach. He leaned back against the cushions and tried to think. Weylin's head, however, ached with all the fury of the worst hangover he could ever remember having, and his hands, moreover, did not feel altogether steady.

Well, Weylin told himself silently as he leaned back with his eyes closed, it seems we were mistaken in Lord Sterne's intentions. How fortunate I've taken Cal's place!

Weylin was scarcely a coward, but it could not be denied that he worried about the coming encounter with Sterne, when the marquis should discover just how his plans had gone awry. The marquis was rumoured to have killed men for far less cause. It did not seem inconceivable to Weylin that Sterne's rage at being thwarted might lead him to do so again.

It really had been naive, Weylin told himself severely, not to have provided himself with a pistol or something of the sort for just this kind of contingency. But he had not, and would therefore just have to watch for his opportunity to escape if need be. At the moment, however, there was nothing he could do. Indeed, a more pressing concern was Melanie's fears. And Cal's, of course. What must they be thinking, that he had not returned by now? And Miss Anthea Marwood? Either she would be fretting over Cal's disappearance or she would have found Calandra and have heard the tale of Weylin's folly. Either way, she must surely be distressed! Glumly Wey began to wonder if he would ever have the chance to see Melanie or Cal or Miss Marwood or his parents again.

Weylin was not often given to such fits of blue devils, but then, he rarely found himself so roughly handled and jolted about. Nor did his head usually ache so abominably! A few minutes of self-pity sufficed to exhaust Weylin's store of patience, and he made an effort to shake off his mood. Cautiously he risked another look out of the window. To his consternation, he saw Sterne signal the driver, and the coach began to slacken its pace. Within a few moments it drew to a halt. Weylin dared not risk another look, but so far as he could recall, the road was deserted of traffic and he had seen no sign of habitations nearby. At all costs, he felt, he must delay his unmasking as long as possible. Carefully but hastily, he arranged the veil over his face. By the time Lord Sterne had opened the door of the coach, Weylin was once more disposed against the cushions as though he were still asleep.

"Well, well, my dear Miss Marwood! Time to awaken," Sterne said silkily as he reached for her.

As Sterne's fingers touched his shoulder, Weylin

pulled away, moving as though he were still half-asleep. Sterne's grip only tightened, however, and he repeated more loudly, "Time, I said, to wake up, Miss Marwood!"

Weylin raised a hand to his head, straightened slightly, then shrank against the cushions as though in alarm. "Frightened?" Lord Sterne laughed. "You've no need to be—just yet! Does your head hurt?" he asked sympathetically. The shrinking figure allowed herself to nod. Sterne clucked. "What a shame. It was necessary, however. I really could not permit a scene, you know. But how else do you feel? Hungry? You'll find some food in the basket over there. Perhaps that will help your headache. I'm afraid I cannot allow you to take your meal in greater comfort, but until we reach our destination, I choose not to risk having you seen." The figure shying away from him made no movement toward the food, and Sterne chuckled. "I really do suggest that you eat, Miss Marwood. We still have a devilish long distance to travel, and I shouldn't wish you to faint from hunger when we arrive."

With a great show of reluctance and an unsteadiness on his feet that was not all pretense, Weylin moved to the opposite side of the coach, next to the basket of food. After another show of hesitation, Wey opened the lid of the basket, wondering if Sterne intended to share this meal. If so, what was Wey to do? The moment he lifted his veil to eat, Sterne would realise that his captive was not Calandra.

But Sterne had other notions in mind. With a wave of his hand the marquis said, "Determined not to speak to me, are you? Never mind. I shan't force my company on you. *Yet.* For now I shall withdraw and leave you to your food." And with another laugh he did so.

Like any young man his age, Weylin was fond of food and always hungry. Whatever qualms he may have had in accepting Lord Sterne's hospitality in this regard were outweighed by the reflection that he would need all his strength in the encounter to come. The contents of the basket had been chosen with the palate of a delicate, frightened young lady in mind. But although Weylin might have preferred fewer sweets and pastries, he did not disdain the slices of roast goose, shaved ham, asparagus, or the bottle of tolerable wine that accompanied it all. So excellent a meal did Weylin make that had Sterne chanced to examine the contents, or lack thereof, of the basket afterward, he must have instantly grown suspicious. But it could not be denied that the food did indeed improve Weylin's headache. And Sterne did not, in any case, show any desire to inspect the basket. In fact, he seemed content to leave his prisoner quite alone. A circumstance for which Weylin was profoundly grateful!

As Weylin relaxed against the cushions, however, his veil once more in place, he began to be aware of another need. One that was steadily growing more urgent. What the devil he was going to do about it, moreover, was beyond him. He couldn't simply open the door of the coach and announce that he had to relieve himself! For one thing, the instant he spoke, Sterne would know Weylin was not Calandra. Wey didn't want to think about what action that revelation might provoke! Still, Weylin's need grew steadily more urgent and he began to think he would indeed have to do something of the sort. Perhaps, Weylin told himself, he could manage a creditable imitation of Cal's voice; after all, they wouldn't be expecting anyone else.

But there was no need. Before Wey had brought himself to the point of acting, the coach door once more opened. It was Lord Sterne, of course. The marquis was still all politeness. "Have you eaten, my dear Miss Marwood? Excellent, excellent. I trust everything was acceptable? Good, good." Lord Sterne paused, then said solicitously, "You must not think, my dear, that I am heedless of your comfort! Indeed, I believe I have thought of everything." "Miss Marwood" did not speak, however, and after a moment Lord Sterne smiled. "No doubt you are too delicately bred to raise such a matter, but if you have not already discovered it, you will find a lady's chamber pot under the seat opposite you. Pray use it, my dear, and when you have done, I shall come back and empty it for you." Still she made no move, and Sterne clucked sympathetically. "So difficult, is it not, my dear, to know what to do? I shall leave you to consider your dilemma. But I warn you, we shall soon be on our way and I do not intend to stop again until well after dawn. So I advise you to overcome your, er, modesty and use the chamber pot!"

And with a bow, Lord Sterne withdrew. Immediately the door was shut behind the marquis, Weylin was on his feet and tugging at the chamber pot, which fit snugly beneath the seat of the

coach. Weylin's need was far too great to allow
of any hesitation on his part. With a sigh he set
it down in the centre of the coach and . . . and
stared at it. How the devil was he to do this in
skirts? It would have been a simple matter, of
course, to lift his skirts up and out of the way.
But Weylin did not trust Lord Sterne. It would
be disastrous were Sterne to suddenly open the
carriage door and discover Weylin. Nor would
Wey put it past the fellow to somehow be watching from a peephole or something!

So, gingerly, Wey settled himself and his skirts
over the lacquered chamber pot and made the
unwelcome discovery that balancing in shoes
that were several sizes too small for his feet
would be no easy task. Eventually, however, the
matter was accomplished and, as fuel to Weylin's
suspicions, Sterne appeared at the coach door
mere moments after he had finished.

A lackey, the driver perhaps, removed the pot
and Sterne regarded his prisoner with eyes that
glittered with desires scarcely held in check. "I
ought, you know, to drug you again," the marquis said with a heavy voice. Weylin shook his
head in alarm, and Sterne considered. "I admit
I am reluctant to do so. It would be better not to
risk a second dose so soon after the first. Nevertheless, I will not have you crying out for help
at every town we pass." Sterne paused again,
this time to allow his captive time to consider
her situation. After a moment he went on. "So
long as you remain silent, I shall permit you to
go undrugged. But I warn you! At the first sign
of trouble on your part, I shall give you enough
to render you unconscious for the rest of our

journey! Is that clear?" Hastily the figure nodded.
"Good. Then I shall leave you, Miss Marwood."
The marquis turned to go, but stopped. With a
puzzled expression he said, "I confess I am somewhat bewildered, Miss Marwood. *Why* did you
wear my brooch? This morning—or rather yesterday morning, by now—you were ready to fling
it back in my face. Swore any gift of mine would
be unacceptable to you! So why, I ask myself,
did you wear it tonight?"

Weylin did not move. He dared not speak, nor
did he dare fling the brooch at his lordship
without speaking. To prolong the conversation
in any way at all was to court disaster. For a
moment the matter hung in the balance. Then
Sterne laughed triumphantly. "I have it! You
cannot be so totally averse to me as you claim
to be. Well, well, what a pleasant surprise indeed!
Frightened but attracted. Perfect! We shall deal
extremely well together, Miss Marwood—Calandra, my dear. I vow I look forward to our marriage more and more all the time! I shall find it
utterly delicious, I assure you!"

Another laugh, and Lord Sterne was, to Weylin's great relief, gone. He could hear the marquis giving orders to the coachman, and soon
they began rattling down the road again. The
carriage was well built, but nothing could have
made the journey a tolerable one for Weylin.
This was, he told himself bluntly, quite the most
outrageous adventure he had ever been part of!
As children, he and Cal had forever been in
mischief together, frightening their parents half
out of their wits at times, and provoking the
most dreadful scolds. Great fun, they had called

it then, and bemoaned the lack of real-life adventures! How delightful it would be, they told themselves, to turn highwaymen and rob coaches when they grew up. Or to go the other route and battle villains! Their games of make-believe had often involved either Wey or Cal being held captive and the other rushing to his or her rescue. It was not so simple, Wey told himself grimly now. Not so simple, nor so much fun. Reality had a bitter taste to it, and Weylin felt as though he had aged ten years in one night.

18

Anthea Marwood and Viscount Radbourne were equally preoccupied. As the night wore on toward dawn, it was evident that they would not soon overtake Lord Sterne and Calandra. The original horses had been changed for another pair, but at none of the posting houses had anything but the most sluggish of nags been available at this time of night. At least that's what they had been told. As the first rays of light began to brighten the sky, Giles spoke to Thea. "In despair, dear one?"

"No." Anthea shook her head resolutely. "So long as they keep travelling, he cannot harm her. And each report we have tells us that they have not stopped."

"She'll be frightened," Giles observed quietly.

Anthea nodded. "Frightened but also angry, I think. Sterne will find Calandra is not a piece of crystal to shatter so easily as he perhaps imagines."

"You are remarkably calm about the matter!"
Giles retorted curtly.

Anthea turned to look at him. "Do you think
so?" she asked with an edge of anger to her
voice. "I suppose it might seem that way to you!
But recollect! I know Calandra. I also know what
it is possible to live through. I wish to God
Calandra could be spared this! But she cannot. I
do not know what the monster will have done to
her by the time we reach them. But I tell you
frankly, Giles, that once we do rescue her, it will
not help the child to act as though she has been
forever scarred. Far better we should reassure
her that no matter what *he* has done, *her* future
will be what she makes of it!"

"Brave words," Giles bit back. "But do you
really think the *ton* will allow it to be so?"

Evenly Anthea answered, "I never said it would
be easy for her, Giles! I only said that *we* must
not allow Cal to give way to despair. There are,
there must always be, solutions, if one allows
oneself the courage to look for them." Giles had
no answer to that, and after a moment Anthea
went on, her voice tinged with scarcely held-
back pain. Giles had to strain to hear her. "Do
you know," she asked, "what is the most frightening part of such a happening? It is the sense
of helplessness. The fear of being set apart forever.
Being crippled by the fear that one can never be
safe again. Hearing sounds in the night and wondering if it is all about to start over again. Knowing there is nowhere to run, that everywhere
there are people to turn and look at you and see
inside your soul and know you're flawed, vulnerable, scarred forever by circumstances you

were helpless to change. Different, set apart, because other people don't bear such scars. Unable to trust because who knows when it will happen again. I know, Giles. Do you wonder that I find it so hard to give up what little control I do have over my own life?"

He shook his head and said gently, "No. But Calandra is not you, nor is her experience quite the same."

Thea nodded. "I know that. Nevertheless, it is enough the same that I tell you we must not allow or encourage her to despair or feel that she is forever scarred. If necessary, I may carry her off to the Continent or ... or *somewhere* until she is once more ready to face the *ton*."

Briefly Giles covered Anthea's hands with one of his own. "With you to help her, my love, I don't doubt Calandra will survive this. You need only lend her a little of your own courage, of which you have so much."

Anthea laughed shakily. "And now you are roasting me, Giles! I haven't half the courage you seem to think I have! Certainly not as much as I would like. Though more, I confess, than before I met you. Oh, Giles, you've been very good for me!"

Radbourne's pulse quickened, and for a moment he couldn't answer. When he did, he spoke lightly. "Well, and so I could say the same for you, dear one. My bailiff tells me that the directions I have sent him for improvements on my properties were long overdue. And my estimable uncle, who is, by the way, as sober as a fish, recently sent me a letter congratulating me on not kicking up a scandal in over two months.

Though that is not, I confess, entirely due to you."

"It isn't?"

Radbourne laughed. "No, it is due, at least in part, to the fact that a number of my boon companions have gone to the Continent in search of adventure."

Soberly Anthea studied Radbourne's face. There was a hint of bitterness about the eyes, and she found herself wanting to stroke it away. Instead she spoke quietly and slowly. "Are you really so very reckless, Giles? You do not seem so to me. I should have said you had a great deal of common sense."

"So I do, when I choose to use it." He shrugged carelessly. "Surely you know my reputation, my love. I have never tried to hide it from you!"

"Yes, I know," she said. "And what I didn't already know, Castor was only too happy to tell me. But I find it difficult to believe what is said about you."

Very deliberately Giles replied, "Well, you should."

Even though he was not looking at her, Anthea shook her head. "No. Oh, I don't doubt you've done all the things Castor told me. What I don't believe is that you're as *hey-go-mad* as they say. Won't you tell me about it now, Giles? We've talked of so many things these past weeks, but you always turn aside from that. There's no need anymore!"

Giles looked down at her and reluctantly smiled. "Very well, dear one. Sometimes I find myself driven by a devil I cannot even put a name to. And when these moods come upon me, I'm primed for any mischief anyone may suggest."

"And yet you are everywhere received," Anthea observed dryly. "Nor, so far as I can discover, have any of these pranks ever hurt anyone save yourself or your foolish companions. You are a fraud, sir!" she said accusingly. "Trying to make me believe you a scapegrace past all redemption! I almost begin to think you wish me to cry off from your offer of marriage!"

"Not in the least, dear one," Giles replied softly, affectionately.

Anthea ignored this treacherous assault on her defenses and said severely, "In point of fact, I would wager that *this* is the most outrageous escapade you've ever engaged in! Spending the night alone with an unmarried young lady. A respectable one," Thea added hastily as Giles looked at her with a gleam of mischief in his eyes.

In answer, Giles reined in the horses and held them easily with one hand. With his other arm, he embraced Anthea. Giles chuckled, then kissed Anthea as she looked at him with an expression of utter astonishment. "Shall we discover just how outrageous we can be?" he demanded roguishly.

She ought, Anthea told herself, as a thoroughly well-bred young woman, to have been appalled. Perhaps even fainted. Certainly, she scolded herself severely, you ought not to be laughing like this! Nor be so depraved as to flutter your lashes at him as you reply provocatively, "Under other circumstances, Giles, I might ask precisely what it is you have in mind. I confess, however, that I cannot help considering it a matter of greater urgency to rescue my niece Calandra!"

Not in the least abashed, Giles released Anthea and once more set the horses going. "Very well, dear one," he said with a gentle laugh. "We shall explore the question later. As soon as we have rescued Cal." To his delight, Anthea answered with a mock growl, and he went on, more soberly, "In point of fact, you have been very good for me, Anthea. My valet, for one, is delighted that these black moods have come upon me scarcely at all since I've met you. Indeed, he tells me he fears I shall dwindle into quite a respectable gentleman if this continues. I need not tell you this is a circumstance both he and my groom would be grateful for!"

Anthea laughed. "No, Giles. Somehow I think that neither you nor I will ever be totally respectable, conventional people. And I thank God for that! I have had a surfeit of such in my life, and there have been times that I felt I was drowning in rules and regulations. I would far rather have someone to laugh with."

"What?" Giles said with mock astonishment. "Are you agreeing to marry me, then?"

"Look to your horses!" she told him severely.

19

The proprietor of the Fox and Hounds inn was leaning against the wall of his establishment, sipping some of his excellent home-brewed ale, when the travelling coach and its outrider pulled into the courtyard. Slowly he straightened, for there was an air about the gentleman on horseback that warned the proprietor that the fellow would expect instant service. As he strode forward, the landlord also noticed the young and very homely lady who peeked from behind the drawn curtains of the coach. Ah, well, not all women could be beauties, could they?

His instincts about the gentleman on horseback were correct, for directly the gentleman espied the proprietor, he said curtly, "You, there. Is there a Mr. Marwood here at the inn?" When the landlord nodded, the gentleman on horseback nodded with satisfaction and said, "Good. You may inform him that Lord Sterne is here."

The landlord was too well-versed in the ways of the gentry to protest such treatment or to risk crossing such a guest. He immediately went inside in search of Mr. Marwood.

Lord Sterne watched him go, then dismounted with a grunt. A night on horseback was enough to tire any man, and Sterne was not so young as he once had been. Nevertheless his step was quite firm as he strode to the travelling coach and pulled open the door. And whatever his feelings, Sterne's voice was schooled to a coaxing silkiness as he said, "What? Still veiled, my dear Calandra? Why, how charming, I protest! But do step down from this carriage. We have arrived at our destination and there is someone here that I am persuaded you will be wishing to see." She hesitated, and Lord Sterne held out his hand peremptorily as he said, "Come! Right now! Or I shall have to help you."

With a slight squaring of his shoulders, Weylin came. He was careful to take mincing steps as they crossed the courtyard, and to rest his gloved hand very lightly on the arm Lord Sterne insisted his captive take. The trembling in that hand was unfeigned, for Weylin was very tired and it seemed to him that this farce must soon reach its climax. Whatever the game, Weylin was determined to see it through so far as he was safely able to.

Inside the inn, the landlord waited with Mr. Marwood. *That* country gentleman was a favoured client of the Fox and Hounds, for whenever Mr. Marwood travelled to Bath to visit his sister, he stopped at the inn for the night. A quiet gentleman, if a trifle particular in his wishes, and one who had never caused the landlord the least amount of trouble. As the young lady and her eldest gentleman companion crossed the threshold of the Fox and Hounds, the young lady gave a cry in a most unladylike voice. "Mr. Marwood! What are you doing here?"

Mouth agape, the landlord watched as the young lady removed her hat and veil to reveal the head of a young man. But if the landlord was confounded, Castor Marwood was even more so. "Weylin Seabrook?" he said, blinking furiously. "With Lord Sterne? Is this indeed so?" The marquis' face was ashen, and he could only nod. Indignantly Marwood exclaimed, "Good God! I had no notion your tastes ran in that direction, my lord! As for you, young Seabrook, I shudder to think what your father will say when he learns you have run off with Lord Sterne! 'Pon my soul, I had no idea how things stood. I would have wagered anything your interest lay in the petticoat sex, my boy. But, my lord, I fail to see why you wanted me to come here to meet you. Or what possessed you to run off with Weylin, when, as your letter informed me, you were on the point of marrying my Cal."

"I did not run off with this boy!" Lord Sterne said through clenched teeth. "I meant to—indeed, I thought I had—run off with your daughter."

"Thought Weylin was Calandra? I never heard of anything so absurd!" Marwood replied. "Why, you'd have had to have windmills in your head to make such a mistake."

"Tell him!" Sterne ordered Wey sharply.

Both men looked at the lad expectantly. It was too much for Weylin, and a sense of unholy delight coursed through him. With mournful eyes he turned to Lord Sterne and said, "How can you say that? You promised I should have anything I wanted—if only I came away with you! All the silks and jewels and skirts I wanted. Why, even this brooch I wear was a gift from you! Can you deny you bought it?"

His eyes almost popping from his head, the proprietor of the Fox and Hounds could bear it no longer. Hastily he intervened. "Gentlemen! Please. A private parlour! That's what you want. A place to talk about this without everyone passing by."

Instantly Castor Marwood seconded the notion. Mopping his brow with a large handkerchief, he said, "Aye, that's the ticket! A private parlour. Surely, my lord, you've no wish to have your business bandied about like this in public?"

The marquis, who looked as though he were about to suffer from apoplexy, made no demur, but merely signalled for the proprietor of the Fox and Hounds to lead the way. Indeed, it seemed to Lord Sterne as though matters were rapidly turning into a nightmare, and he was grateful for the few minutes of confusion to try to gather his thoughts. As the landlord closed the door behind the three members of the *ton*, Lord Sterne began once more an ineffectual explanation.

Shaking his head, the proprietor retreated to the courtyard. Never in a hundred years would he understand the ways of Quality! The landlord didn't have much time, however, to consider them before a curricle and pair drove into view. Ah, more customers, the landlord thought with pleasure. His pleasure changed to doubt as he realised that the lady in the curricle was Mr. Marwood's maiden sister. Sitting mighty close she was to the gentleman driving, and not a groom or abigail to be seen anywhere. Somehow the landlord's instincts warned him that he was not going to have a quiet morning after all! Nevertheless, Miss Anthea Marwood had always seemed a perfect lady to him, and the habit of respectfulness toward her was still very strong. The proprietor therefore hastened forward to say, "You're here, I doubt not, to see your brother. I'll take you right inside to find him, and my boy, George, will see to your horses, sir."

Anthea blinked at this unexpected speech and turned to Giles, certain that she could not have heard correctly. Soothingly he patted her hand and gravely thanked the innkeeper. As they followed the fellow inside, Giles told Thea softly, "If they are not here, we shall go on immediately, I promise you."

Without ceremony, the innkeeper threw open the door of the private parlour to reveal Marwood, Weylin, and Lord Sterne deep in acrimonious conversation. In the abrupt silence that fell, Lord Sterne's voice rang out: "Anthea Marwood and Viscount Radbourne. It only wanted that!"

For their part, Thea and Giles could only stare in amazement at the trio. Finally Thea found her voice to demand, "Where is Calandra?"

It was Weylin who answered. "With Melanie Balder. In Bath."

The spell was broken. "*Anthea Marwood*!" Castor thundered. "What the devil are you doing here? And in the company of *that* man?"

Hastily the innkeeper retreated, closing the door of the private parlour behind him. Whatever the discussion was going to be, he didn't want to know about it. It never paid to get involved in the quarrels of the Quality!

Anthea waited until the proprietor was gone; then she spoke quietly, determined to ignore the accusation in Castor's voice. "We came to rescue *your* daughter from Lord Sterne," Thea said bluntly. "Though I now perceive that there was no need for me to do so. Very clever of you, Weylin! Or was it Calandra's notion for you to take her place?"

"Mine," he retorted indignantly.

"Clever?" Castor demanded. "You're pleased to see the boy here with Lord Sterne? Have your wits gone begging?"

No one paid Marwood the slightest heed as Radbourne observed dryly, "It was either very clever or very foolhardy, Seabrook. Perhaps both! Suppose Sterne had taken you to some deserted house? Do you really imagine you would have been a match for him? Particularly in skirts?"

"I . . . I never thought he would try to abduct me—Cal, I mean," Weylin stammered. "I . . . I overheard him tell Mrs. Taggert he only intended to put a fright into Cal."

"Abduct my Calandra? *Abduct* her?" Castor Marwood said with an air of bewilderment. "But I thought you said you ran away with his lordship because he promised you all manner of things, Seabrook."

"Oh, shut up!" Sterne flung at Castor testily.

"Must you be an absolute fool? I meant to abduct your daughter and bring her here. To you. Since she would have spent the night in my company, between us we could have forced her marriage to me by Special License. I have one in my pocket. A license, I mean."

"But instead you spent the night with Weylin? Cold comfort that must have been!" Giles observed with no little amusement. "Sometime you must tell me how it is you failed to notice the difference. If you were indeed close enough to compromise Miss Marwood's honour!" Weylin's face held a look of outrage and he would have spoken hotly had Giles not held up a hand to forestall him. Silkily Giles went on, "I suggest you leave England for a while, Lord Sterne. Perhaps visit the Continent, or even cross the Atlantic. But in any event, you are to leave Miss Calandra Marwood alone. If I hear of your annoying her or any of her friends or family again, I shall make it my business to see that the story of last night's escapade becomes the latest *on-dit* among the *ton*. Somehow I don't imagine you would like that very well."

For a moment Lord Sterne could only stand there regarding Radbourne with an expression of rage. Finally he bowed, however, and said, "Very well. I shall go. But someday, Radbourne, there shall be a reckoning between us!"

Giles also bowed. "I look forward to that day," he said simply.

Sterne turned on his heel and left, slamming the door of the private parlour behind him. Anthea could not help but shiver. "Don't be afraid, my dear," Giles said, putting an arm around her. "I assure you there is no need to be."

"By Jove, you're a regular Trojan, sir!" Weylin exclaimed.

Marwood was not so pleased. "Unhand my sister!" he thundered. "I must be grateful that you tried to come to my daughter's rescue, even if, as it appears, her rescue was totally unnecessary. Gratitude cannot compel me, however, to condone your unwelcome attentions toward my sister!"

"Unwelcome attentions?" Weylin repeated, puzzled. "They don't seem unwelcome to me."

"Young man," Castor said with an air of outrage, "I advise *you* to be silent!"

"*Unwelcome?*" Anthea demanded.

"Hush, my love," Giles told her soothingly. "Marwood, I find your words and tone offensive. But perhaps you are unaware that your sister is about to become my wife?"

Castor permitted himself to laugh. "Whatever other follies my sister may allow herself to commit, I am persuaded that marriage to a man such as yourself is not among them."

"You seem very certain of that," Giles observed mildly.

"I am." Marwood permitted himself a slight bow. "I fancy myself to be a man of common sense. My sister has always had the highest regard for propriety, and although she has a streak of levity about her that I cannot like, I find it impossible to believe that she could so far forget herself as to marry a man who is an acknowledged rake. Absolutely out of the question, I assure you! Isn't it, Anthea, my dear?"

Anthea's eyes glittered dangerously as she regarded her brother. Softly she said, "Propriety? Tell me, brother. *If* Lord Sterne had succeeded in his plot, and brought Calandra here instead of Weylin Seabrook, what would you have done?"

"Told her to marry him, of course," Castor replied uneasily. "Nothing else to have been done, would there? And I must say that I take it very unkindly that young Seabrook saw fit to interfere. Otherwise we might have had it fixed up all right and tight between us by now."

"And what of Calandra's feelings?" Anthea demanded hotly.

"Feelings? Nonsense!" Castor retorted just as hotly. "Her feelings matter no more than yours do. Mere missishness! She'd soon have gotten over it, I promise you! Permit me to say that I know more of the world than you do, my dear Anthea, and that for my daughter to follow in your footsteps and become a spinster—an ape-leader—is totally repugnant to me! Perhaps you like being called an eccentric, but would my Cal? I'll not have her whistle her future—ruin it—merely because she is timid or shy! And furthermore, with two sisters yet left at home to provide for, and funds at low tick, I should have thought she would show less selfishness. Where am I to find another suitor for my Cal with such a title and as well-heeled as Lord Sterne? He don't show it in his clothes or manners or habits, but Sterne's one of the richest men in England. Aye, and with a title that goes back a long ways!"

"But Cal don't care about such things!" Weylin protested.

Patiently Marwood replied, "That is because Calandra is very young and very foolish."

Radbourne coughed politely. "Will it make my suit more acceptable to you, Marwood, if I point out that I, too, have a title and am well-heeled?"

"You?" Castor was visibly affronted. "What the devil good does that do me? I don't get any money from it if you marry my sister. But Sterne! His lordship was kind enough to offer to forgo a dowry. Aye, and pay me a handsome sum on the side, as well."

With an effort, Anthea dragged her brother's attention back to the matter at hand. "Castor," she said patiently, "if you believe Calandra would have had no choice but to marry Lord Sterne, then surely you agree that I have no choice but to marry Radbourne. After all, I spent the night with him in his curricle."

Castor permitted himself to smile and wag a finger playfully at Thea. "Now, now, my dear! An open curricle is scarcely a likely place for scandalous behaviour. Particularly for a woman your age. While I cannot like the expedition, I would only call it foolish. To say more would be to refine too much upon the matter. No, I could not call it sufficiently scandalous as to require your marriage to Radbourne."

"I would," Weylin said hopefully.

Everyone ignored him. "Tell me, Marwood," Giles asked curiously, "why are you so opposed to your sister's marriage? I should have thought it could only add to your credit to see her well established."

Marwood nodded vigorously. "And so it would!

But I fancy that my sister's welfare ranks higher in my concern than what credit her status holds for me. Nor do I object to marriage for her. Why, my wife, Eugenia, has taken great pains to bring any number of eligible gentlemen to Anthea's attention. A kindness for which, I am sorry to say, my sister has shown not the least gratitude. But so it is, and I shall not scold her for it." Marwood paused, took a deep breath, and then plunged on. "Even disregarding my wife's efforts, had Anthea shown the least desire to settle down with a steady gentleman of reliable habits and untarnished reputation, I should not have stood in her way. But *you*, sir! I'm a plain man and I'll speak bluntly. You stand for everything I find repugnant! The only way I would ever agree to her marriage to you is if I were to find that she was as depraved as your reputation brands you to be! And believe me, Radbourne, I shall take pains to be sure that you have no chance to further corrupt her. Have I made my meaning sufficiently clear?"

"You have," Giles said with a voice as brittle as ice.

"You can't say such things to him!" Weylin protested.

"Considering how I find you dressed," Marwood told the boy levelly, "be grateful I don't speak my mind to you!" He then turned to his sister. "And you, my dear. Will you forget this madness? Renounce Radbourne? Swear you will never see him again?" Vehemently Thea shook her head, and Castor persisted impatiently. "You must believe that I know what is best for you!

Marriage to a man like Radbourne would mean a lifetime of misery for you."

Anthea turned to look at Giles. When she spoke, it was so softly that her brother could scarcely hear her. "And life without him would be an eternity of intolerable loneliness."

But this was too much for Weylin, in spite of his sympathy for the pair. "Good God!" he snorted. "You all sound like characters out of a Cheltenham tragedy! As if you needed to listen to such fustian, Miss Marwood. You're of age, and so is Radbourne. What difference does it make what Mr. Marwood thinks? What *I* want to know is what *we're* going to do next."

"I, for one, am going to return to Bath and retrieve Calandra," Anthea said decisively. "I hope Melanie had the sense to confide in her mother! Letty will be shrewd enough to see to it that Cal goes about in public today, so that everyone knows she is still in Bath. Giles, how soon may we leave here?"

"Tomorrow," was Radbourne's prompt reply. "Or the day after."

"Tomorrow?" Anthea repeated incredulously. "You must be roasting me! I intend to start back today. Within the hour, if possible!"

"But it is not possible, my love," Giles told her firmly.

"Indeed not!" Marwood agreed in shocked tones. "She will return to Bath with me, and I most certainly will not be ready to start out until tomorrow at the earliest. Why, even if the horses were put to at once, we could not possibly reach Bath until well after nightfall. And I tell you frankly, my sleep last night was cut up quite enough as it was!"

Weylin nobly threw himself into the breach. "I shall take you back to Bath today, Miss Marwood."

"You?" Marwood demanded in outrage. "Why, you're even more disreputable now than *he* is! What if someone should see my sister with you? Good God, the notion of Anthea jaunting about the countryside with a young man dressed up in skirts staggers the mind!"

As Weylin coloured furiously, Giles asked gently, "Forgive me, Weylin, Anthea, but does either of you possess sufficient funds for such a journey?"

Slowly Thea and Weylin looked at one another, then shook their heads. "I didn't think to open my strongbox before I came," Anthea said quietly.

Weylin stammered, "If . . . if you will lend me the funds, sir, I promise I shall pay you back as soon as I have drawn a draft on my account in Bath." He paused, shot a resentful glance at Marwood, and added, "If you could spare enough, sir, I should also like to purchase some decent clothes to ride back in."

"You certainly do need other clothes, and I shall see that you have them," Radbourne agreed. "But you will not be returning to Bath today. Tomorrow or, more likely, the day after, I shall hire a horse for you, Seabrook, and you may ride alongside the curricle with Anthea and myself."

"But, Giles—" Anthea protested impatiently.

Without the least haste, Giles possessed himself of both of Anthea's hands. "Hush, dear one," he told her soothingly. "You've said yourself that Mrs. Balder does not want for sense. She will take excellent care of Calandra until we return, and if you wish, we shall send her a message at once letting her know what has occurred. And telling her and Cal and Melanie that you and Weylin are quite all right." Once more Thea would have protested, but Giles went on, seriously, "Believe me, beloved, that I would take you back at once if I thought there was the least need. But there is not, and you are pale with fatigue. You must rest, and I will not have you jaunting about the countryside until you have had some sleep and are looking quite yourself again."

Weylin nodded approvingly. "I must say, that makes sense," he told Anthea. "And that will give me time to get some other clothes. Only, I think sir," he said a trifle doubtfully, looking at Radbourne, "that you'd better purchase them for me."

Giles nodded, and even Castor was moved to say, "You'd best listen to him, Anthea. Sensible notions he's had there. *Not* that I agree to my sister's return to Bath in your company, sir. *I* shall take her home!"

Anthea's eyes flashed with anger, and there is no knowing what she might have said to her brother had Giles not intervened. "You'd best go and write that note for Mrs. Balder," he told her firmly.

Anthea hesitated and finally nodded. "Very well. And since it is inevitable, I shall speak to the landlord and arrange for our rooms."

If the door of the private parlour did not slam as it closed behind Anthea, it was nevertheless evident that she had used unbecoming force in shutting it. The three men turned to one another, and after a moment, Radbourne and Seabrook were deep in discussion of what precisely the young man would require in the way of attire. Disgusted, Marwood withdrew.

20

There was a small spinney a short distance down
the road from the Fox and Hounds inn, and that
was where Lord Radbourne discovered Miss
Marwood several hours later. "Anthea?"

Startled, she looked up. "How did you find
me?" she asked.

For a moment Giles stared at the lovely face
that looked out at him from beneath a green
poke bonnet and clusters of red curls. Finally he
shrugged. "The landlord's wife told me you had
gone out. I looked around and wondered where
you might go to sort out your thoughts."

"How well you know me!" Anthea exclaimed.

Radbourne shook his head. "Not yet, but I
shall, someday. I came to tell you that I've sent
off that note to Mrs. Balder." He paused, then
asked quietly, "Still fretting over Calandra?"

"Do you know," Anthea replied with a slight
smile, "I wasn't thinking of Calandra at all! I
was wondering what people will think when I

marry you. How many will be shocked. If Castor truly will cast me off. That sort of thing."

"One person, at least, will be pleased," Giles answered quietly. As Anthea looked at him enquiringly, Giles went on, "Letty Balder. She once told me that she thought I could bring you happiness. And, as you've often told me, she doesn't want for sense." He paused and the smile left his face. Seriously he asked, "Are you trying to tell me, dear one, that you've changed your mind? That you're afraid to marry me?"

"I have always been afraid of marriage," Anthea answered simply. "Nor have I ever tried to hide that fact from you."

Miss Marwood lowered her eyes and seemed to find great interest in the buttons of the viscount's satin waistcoat. Giles found himself presented with the top of Thea's green bonnet to stare at, and one stray curl that had escaped to nestle against the curve of her neck. He fought the urge to toss away the bonnet and unpin the rest of her curls. Instead, Giles took her hands in his and said, "Are you telling me, my love, that you wish to cry off?"

Suddenly Anthea looked up at Giles, and a mischievous smile transformed her face. "Oh, no, my lord! My backbone seems to have stiffened admirably since you entered my life, and I'm not about to sacrifice what I have gained. Most certainly *not* for Castor's precious sense of propriety!"

The laughter in Radbourne's eyes matched that in hers as he replied, "I'm very glad to hear it, dear one, for I swear I should not have let you go! Indeed, I was beginning to feel a certain sympathy with Sterne. Wondering if I ought, perhaps, to make plans to spirit *you* away."

Anthea laughed but then grew sober again. "How I wish it could be so simple, Giles!" He started to speak, and she cut him short. "No, don't worry. I don't mean to indulge in a fit of the megrims. I'm not such a poor creature as that! I shall, moreover, marry you when and where you wish, and let the world say what it will."

Giles released one of Anthea's hands so that he might stroke her cheek. "I fancy Marwood exaggerates the problem, dear one," he told her. "Whatever your brother may say, and whatever activities I may have indulged in in the past, I wager there are very few members of the *ton* who will choose to cut you once we are wed. A title and wealth do wonders for one's credit, and I swear to you that Marwood's fears that you will be a social leper have no truth outside his head!"

"Then why—?"

Giles shook his head impatiently. "I don't know! Oh, I've no doubt your brother believes what he says and that he has indeed convinced himself that he holds your best interests at heart. Nevertheless, in this he is a fool."

Once more Anthea looked away. "That's all very well," she said reluctantly, "but suppose he chooses to take Cal away from me? He might very well, you know."

"Does it matter so very much anymore?" Giles asked, puzzled.

"Matter?" Anthea exploded angrily. "Of course it matters! I've promised I shall protect her."

"Protect her from what?" Giles asked sensibly. "I doubt very, very much that Lord Sterne will approach her again."

"Yes, but . . . but what if her parents try to marry her to someone else like him?" Anthea persisted.

Giles regarded her steadily. "Last night, my love, *you* told me that Calandra was not a piece of crystal to shatter so easily. And spending these past weeks with you in Bath will have strengthened her even further. Unless you and I are much mistaken in our belief in her, Calandra will never allow herself to be forced into a distasteful marriage."

"I suppose you're right," Anthea conceded reluctantly. Suddenly she laughed. "Indeed, when I stop to think about it, it really is too bad of me to think of Cal as a helpless child! She is rapidly turning into a lovely, sensible, forcible woman."

"Good." Giles nodded approvingly. "Any other reservations?" he asked teasingly. She hesitated, and he suggested, "Maggie?" Reluctantly Anthea nodded, and Giles tightened his grip on her hands. "I swear to you that Mrs. Taggert means nothing to me anymore. As for the future, I cannot imagine that, having you, I could ever desire any other woman!"

"Nor I another man," she said.

"Do you know the Robert Herrick poem?" Giles asked. "*To Anthea, Who May Command Him Anything?*"

Puzzled, Anthea nodded. "My mother was used to read it to me. But I never understood," she added mischievously, "what good it could do *her* to have him languish away or . . . or give way to despair under some stupid tree! Or why any man would be such a simpleton as to do so merely because his ladylove asked him to. One would think it would give him a disgust of her selfishness!"

Giles laughed aloud. "My dear, sweet, sensible one! Very well, let us ignore those verses. Nevertheless, this one holds true, and I wish you to know that it does. *Thou art my life, my love, my heart,/The very eyes of me,/And has command of every part,/To live and die for thee.*"

He would have kissed her then and there were it not for the voice calling out, "Miss Marwood! Lord Radbourne!"

"Weylin," Anthea said with a groan.

"Someone," Giles said with feeling, "is going to strangle that young pup one of these days!" Nevertheless he called out, "We're in here, Seabrook. What the devil do you want?"

"Marwood has ordered tea for us all. Sent me to fetch you," the boy explained as he entered the spinney, following their voices.

Resigned to the ways of fate, Giles and Anthea went to meet him, and the three headed back to the inn. "I see you've changed to the clothes I bought you," Giles told Weylin. "How do they fit?"

"A trifle tight, but far better than that dress of Cal's!" Weylin retorted with a grin.

"I'm sorry, but it was the best I could do," Giles apologised. "This *is* a rather small town, you know."

"Oh, I ain't complaining," Weylin said cheerfully. "I wouldn't have missed this adventure for the world. It's beyond anything great, isn't it, Miss Marwood?"

"Oh, beyond anything," Anthea agreed faintly.

"I knew you were a right 'un," Wey told her approvingly. "Mind you, there were moments last night when I wasn't at all sure about the whole business, but everything's worked out for the best, after all. Cal will be green with envy that she missed all the fun. You do understand, don't you, Miss Marwood!"

"Certainly," she assured the boy resolutely. "Why, the thought of the whole affair and your part in it makes me feel quite green as well!"

"I know." Weylin nodded sympathetically. "It must have been dreadfully tame merely riding after us in a curricle. Next time p'rhaps we can arrange for *you* to take Cal's place instead of me. How's that?"

With strong feelings, Anthea retorted, "I devoutly hope, Weylin Seabrook, that there will *never* be another such time. And if there is, I can only hope that I am miles away and discover it many years later—if ever!"

Weylin was too polite to say what he thought of such poor-spiritedness, but he could not entirely hide his disillusionment in Miss Marwood's character. "Don't worry," Giles told the boy soothingly. "She'll be herself, all ripe for adventure again, after a sound night's sleep."

Weylin brightened visibly at this and Anthea's feelings threatened to overcome her. But the Fox and Hounds was in sight now, as was Castor Marwood's visage peering from a parlour window. Sighting the party, he beckoned impatiently to them. Once they were inside, he had a great deal more to add. "So, Weylin, you found them together, I suppose? You really ought to take better care of your reputation, sister. What our dear Papa would have said, I cannot imagine. But there! I don't mean to pinch at you. Come and eat. The Fox and Hounds sets a tolerable tea, a tolerable tea indeed. Anthea, you may pour. Milk and sugar, you know."

Anthea did as she was bid, exchanging a look of amusement with Giles. Weylin was a trifle more doubtful but in the end decided there was no point in disputing such cavalier treatment. Which was, perhaps, just as well.

Under the influence of the excellently prepared food, Castor Marwood began to mellow. He pronounced his sister a "good girl" and Weylin "merely a young lad of high spirits in need of a steady head to guide him." As he went on, however, to advise Thea to place herself in Eugenia's capable hands if she wished to find a husband, and offered to provide the steady head he said Weylin needed, Marwood scarcely endeared himself to the pair. Only Radbourne seemed quite comfortable. To Anthea's affronted eyes it was evident, in fact, that Giles was greatly enjoying himself and even encouraging Castor's more outrageous pronouncements! As the day wore on, matters only, in Thea's opinion, grew worse, and she and Weylin sought their beds early, neither in the best of humour.

Several hours later, as Marwood and Radbourne sat amiably together, sharing a decent brandy, Castor was moved to say, "A pity marriage between you and m'sister is out of the question."

"A great pity," Giles agreed.

"By Jove, I quite begin to think I like you!" Castor said, slapping the table with his hand. "Mind you, I shan't change my mind. My duty to Anthea is clear, and I shall abide by it. Eugenia will see to that," he concluded gloomily.

"Your wife," Giles observed sympathetically.

"Yes, my wife," Marwood agreed. "Haven't met her, have you? Wonderful woman. That's what everyone says, especially her. Powerfully set on duty, aye, and appearance as well. Won't hear of the least breath of scandal about any of us. Not even when it's just flirting with an opera dancer," Castor confided.

Giles, who had also been dipping rather deeply into the brandy, leaned forward. "Tell me, Marwood," he said in a voice scarcely above a whisper, "how comes it about that a woman as stiff-rumpled—I mean, of the highest principles—as Mrs. Marwood would countenance a match between a man as notorious as the Marquis of Sterne and her daughter?"

Castor also leaned forward and touched the tip of his nose with a forefinger. "Excellent question," he conceded. "There was the money, of course, and the title. But the real reason is that Eugenia and I never much liked the girl. Too clever, by half, my Calandra! Wanted her off our hands as quickly as possible. She's not quiet and biddable like our other girls. She's been a source of one trouble after another as long as I can remember, Cal has. To tell the truth, I've a mind to let her stay with Anthea as long as m'sister is willing to have her. No matter what Eugenia says!" Castor paused and considered the matter. "Of course," he said fairly, "I daresay Genia will agree, so long as m'sister is willing to keep on franking the girl."

"But your duty . . .?" Giles suggested delicately.

Marwood winked, then chuckled. "Ah, that's the beauty of it, don't you see? Anthea will see to Cal's needs and her comeout and all, and we needn't think we're neglecting her. Damme, but I wish there were some way to fix it up all right and tight between you and my sister!" As Giles blinked at this abrupt change of subject, Marwood went on mournfully, "Aye, but there ain't. And when I'm sober, I suppose I'll be glad of it. Doubt I'll ever remember this conversation. Not," he said sharply, "that I'm *castaway* just now. Only a bit *on the go*. Still, I think it's time I sought my bed. Good night, Radbourne."

Giles stood to watch Marwood weave his way unsteadily to the door. A half-formed plan began to fill his mind, and soon after that Giles rang for the boot boy. After he had spoken with the lad, he sent for the landlord himself. Giles was, he thought, being quite discreet. It is indisputable, however, that had he been more sober, Giles would never have put his plan into effect.

21

Anthea came awake slowly, stretching and trying to force open her rebellious eyes. It had been well after midnight when she fell asleep, in spite of her lack of rest the previous night, when they were, as she had thought, trying to rescue Cal. The bed was a large one and Thea was still stretching with her eyes closed when abruptly she stopped. Gingerly her hand explored the object beside her in the bed. It was a body! Anthea's eyes flew open and she yanked the bedsheets up to her chin. A man, a naked man, was asleep in her bed! It wasn't happening, it couldn't be. Anthea eased herself to the side of the bed, prepared to scream, when a muffled voice came from the body. "*Please* don't do that! I've the devil of a head this morning."

"Giles!" Anthea said, outraged.

Radbourne, who had been lying on his stomach on top of the covers, his head turned away from her, lifted his head and smiled engagingly at Thea. "Who else did you think might be in your bed, my love?"

Before Anthea could do more than bristle at these words a knock sounded at the door and a fuzzy voice demanded, "Anthea? What's going on?"

"Come in and find out," Giles replied loudly.

"No!" Anthea shouted. But it was too late. "Castor!" she gasped faintly as her brother entered the room.

Hastily Marwood shut the door behind him before anyone else should discover the appalling sight that met his eyes. "Anthea!" he said, his eyes protruding. "The boot boy said you had need of me, but I had no notion ..." For a moment he was at a loss for words; then he went on, "Viscount Radbourne! And my sister! In bed together! I can scarcely believe my eyes. Have you no sense of shame? Either of you? Eugenia warned me how it would be, but I was fool enough to say that my sister had more sense than to ever allow herself to be compromised in such a way!"

"Do you mean," Giles asked, wide-eyed, propping himself up on one elbow, "that your wife predicted that I would one day be found in Anthea's bed?"

Hastily Castor averted his eyes. "For God's sake, cover yourself up, Radbourne!" he thundered.

"All right," Giles replied cheerfully as he lifted the covers and slid beneath them.

"That is *not* what I meant," Castor shouted.

"I know," Giles agreed sympathetically. "But perhaps your wife might have foreseen that also?"

Mr. Marwood glared at the viscount. Finally he mastered himself enough to say from between clenched teeth, "You misunderstood me, sir. I did not mean to imply that my wife ever expected me to find my sister between the sheets with a man! I only meant that she had warned me of the dangers of a young woman alone."

"But if Anthea were truly alone right now," Giles pointed out reasonably, "there would be no need for concern, would there?"

"You may consider this a jesting matter," Castor replied, "but rest assured that *I* do not! I cannot and will not stand by and see my sister treated so. If you had any notion of seducing and then abandoning my sister, you may forget such a thing. *You* may treat your conquests lightly, but I do not. If you do not acknowledge the wrong you have done Anthea, I shall take steps to ensure that you will. My sister may have been imprudent and perhaps far worse. If so, I am sorry for it, but that in no way lessens your responsibility to make amends, Lord Radbourne."

But this was too much for Anthea. The covers were forgotten as she leaned forward to demand softly, "Castor, what are you doing in my bedchamber? Particularly at such an hour of the morning? Do you make it a practice to arrive unannounced?"

Mr. Marwood stiffened even as he stammered, "I . . . I told you. The boot boy brought me a message that my sister required my assistance, and what's more, I should consider that he was quite right! To find you in bed with one whom I can only call a hardened libertine! Certainly I would rather believe that you sent for me than that my own sister is no better than a piece of haymarket wares!"

Slowly, evenly, Anthea said, "Who are you to judge me, Castor? A man who would have married his daughter to that satyr, Lord Sterne!"

"Now, Anthea, you have no right to question my authority over Calandra," Marwood began firmly.

With a complete disregard for the proprieties, oblivious of her cap and high-necked, long-sleeved nightgown, Anthea Marwood climbed out of bed and advanced on her brother. "And *you* have no right to be in my bedchamber. Get out! Get out at once, do you hear me!"

Castor held up a hand. "I'll go. But only as far as the nearest minister. You'll marry Lord Radbourne, Anthea, as soon as it can be managed. However careless of your reputation you may be, I am not."

Giles, who was enjoying the scene hugely, called from the bed, "Excellent notion, Marwood! I even have the Special License in my pocket."

Anthea turned and looked at Giles. "In your pocket?" she asked.

Giles had the grace to colour. "Well, in my room, anyway. I've had it these two weeks past, now. You should have no trouble finding a cleric to tie the knot, Marwood. I suggest you begin at once."

Castor looked at Radbourne and said grimly. "You may well laugh at me, my lord, but under no other circumstances would I have allowed my sister to marry you! Good day. I shall be back as soon as I have found that minister. By then I trust you will be back in your own room."

Anthea closed the door behind the furious Marwood and then advanced on the bed. Viscount Radbourne was lying there, hands behind his head, smiling at her. "How dare you?" she demanded furiously.

"Why, your brother told you," Giles said innocently. "I'm a hardened libertine."

In answer, Anthea Marwood so far forgot her dignity as to seize a feather pillow and beat Lord Radbourne about the head with it. They struggled as he laughed. And somehow, a few minutes later, Anthea found herself in Radbourne's arms, caught up in an embrace that she welcomed as much as he did. Later, Anthea could not have said whether it was his fingers or hers that tossed away her cap. "Why did you do this?" she asked, her head tucked under his chin and resting on his chest.

Giles kissed the top of Thea's head. "Because I was drunk. And your brother was talking such nonsense about honour and duty and propriety. I guess I decided to put matters into perspective for him."

"Villain," she murmured as she snuggled closer. "But what was he saying about the boot boy?"

"I was rather drunk, you understand," Giles explained apologetically, "but I recall something about asking the boot boy to rouse Marwood early this morning and tell him that you required his assistance."

"And how did you get into my room?" Anthea asked suspiciously.

"Well, you must recollect that this *is* the Fox

and Hounds," Giles said with wide, innocent eyes. "The landlord is most discreet!"

Grimly Anthea reached once more for the pillows. Laughing, she and Giles struggled together until, breathless, Anthea said without rancour, "You utter, utter beast! Now what?"

"Now what?" Giles repeated, staring down into her eyes with a curious smile. "I estimate we have about two hours before your brother returns with that prelate. Let's not waste them."

About the Author

April Lynn Kihlstrom was born in Buffalo, New York, and graduated from Cornell University with an M.S. in Operations Research. She, her husband, and their two children enjoy traveling and have lived in Paris, Honolulu, Georgia, and New Jersey. When not writing, April Lynn Kihlstrom enjoys needlework and devotes her time to handicapped children.

SIGNET Regency Romances You'll Enjoy